About the Author

Frank Dirscherl is the author of many novels, including the Amazon bestselling *The Wraith* and *Sanderson of Metro,* as well as several short stories. His *The Wraith Dread Avenger of the Underworld* books have been enjoyed by readers all over the world.

A librarian with over thirty years experience, Frank has also worked at a book wholesaler, a specialist medical practice and as a tutor in the writing and producing of comic books. His interests include reading, traveling, politics, architecture and the environment.

Frank lives in the Illawarra on the south coast of New South Wales, Australia, with his wife and daughter, and is always working on his latest literary endeavors.

GLOWING EYES MEDIA

Praise for *Sanderson of Metro*
Amazon bestseller

"Once shrouded in mystery, The Wraith's stunning origin is finally revealed. Dirscherl and Nash have written one hell of an adventure novel filled with myth, intrigue, and excitement. Highly recommended reading."

- A.P. Fuchs, writer, *The Axiom-man Saga, The Way of the Fog, Undead World trilogy*

"Recommended for Wraith and pulp hero fans."

– Leon Mallett, *Amazon*

"At the end of the day, this novel is a worthy addition to The Wraith's continuing story and a necessary purchase if you're a fan of the character. It's also just a flat out enjoyable reading experience."

– Marcus Bucklin, *Amazon*

"The story is well written, and the Paul Sanderson character fleshed out fairly well...I highly recommend this well written entry for all comic book fans."

– Virginia E. Johnson, *Amazon*

Praise for *The Wraith*
Amazon bestseller

"I love the coloring job and specially the 'glowing' eyes on the chest of the character."
- Guillermo del Toro, director, *Blade II, Hellboy I & II*

"I liked the story a lot... It's a very strong debut."
Steve Englehart, writer, *Detective Comics, The Avengers, Green Lantern*

"I have read the novel (I couldn't put it down)... It is amazing to see how her (Leena) character evolves from Part I to Part II. At first she appears as every other 'girlfriend' in an action film, but those twelve months that pass obviously change her as a person and I love the person she becomes: tougher, but still human."
- Amber Moelter, actress, *Catwoman: Copycat*

"I finished *The Wraith* book last night. I must say I enjoyed it quite a bit. The scenes kept playing in my head like a big budget Hollywood film. I mentioned earlier that I enjoy when the hero is put to the test physically and doesn't win the battle unscathed. Boy, (Frank) delivered that in spades!"
- Jeff Welborn, artist, *Nightmare World, The Wraith*

"Genius + sweat + dedication = hard hittin' hero action! Go Aussie!"
- Dan Lennard, writer, *People* magazine

"*The Wraith* is a wonderful throwback to the purple prose of the bloody pulps with a hero clearly descendant from the likes of the Shadow and the Spider. A fast, action-packed thrill-ride with great characters, both noble and villainous. Slam-bang kick off to a super new series. One I'm anxious to follow."
  – Ron Fortier, writer, *The Spider, Brother Bones, Domino Lady*

"I became familiar with Frank Dirscherl's The Wraith from the comic book of the same name. When the first Wraith novel came out I just had to read it. I was not disappointed. The Wraith is a fast-paced thrill-ride. I'm looking forward to the upcoming sequel."
  – Bobby Nash, writer, *Evil Ways, Fantastix, Lance Star*

"*The Wraith* (is) a really fun read. Have been a fan of Kenneth Robeson's Doc Savage and The Avenger books for years... *The Wraith* reminds me of Robeson at his best."
  – G.R. Lawson, Publisher, General Jinjur Comics

"A short, pulp, superhero novel... Clearly more adventures to come with how this is set up."
  – Richard Scott, *Super Reader* website

"*The Wraith* is an enlightening journey into the darkness of superhero fiction, and a worthy entry into both pulpdom and comicdom."
  – Kevin Noel Olson, *Silver Bullet Comics* website

Praise for *Valley of Evil*

"The second Wraith novel is an improvement, I think. Right from the start Dirscherl throws you into the middle of crazy action.... This book is a whole lot of superheroic pulp fun, and the good news is there seems to be more to come...I look forward to some more of the same."

> – Richard Scott, *Super Reader* website

"I think (Dirscherl) really captured a noir element with (his) voice."

> – Joshua Gamon, writer, *Abigail & Rox, Digital Webbing Presents*

"I did quite enjoy the books. Best of all, it wasn't overly sex-filled or gory—I can't stand most modern superhero comics that show such things or have the heroes just swear and swear. So *The Wraith* (and *Valley of Evil*) was just up my alley."

> – Greg Gick, writer, *The Werewolf of Rutherford Grange, Tales of the Shadowmen, Secret Agent X Vol. 2*

"The Dread Avenger is back. After battling the Cobra in his first prose adventure, The Wraith returns to face all new challenges from Metro City's greatest villains, most notably Hong Kong drug kingpin Ma Tzi. As with his first Wraith novel, Frank Dirscherl treats us to a pulp-inspired adventure that keeps readers on the edge of their seat. You have to read this novel in one sitting."

> – Bobby Nash, writer, *Evil Ways, Fantastix, Lance Star*

"In the past five years there has been a tremendous resurgence in pulp fiction centering on the old heroic pulps. Young writers have started taking up the mantle of old masters like Walter Gibson and Lester Dent and begun creating their own avengers in tales of genuine purple prose. Among the best of this new generation of wordsmiths is Australian, Frank Dirscherl and the exploits of his modern pulp paladin, The Wraith. This is grand pulp!"

   – Ron Fortier, writer, *The Spider, Brother Bones, Domino Lady*

Praise for *Crossfire*

"Stephen did a fantastic job of bringing Frank Dirscherl's character to life!"
- Adam DiTroia, composer, *The Wraith: Eyes of Judgment*,
MTV, Fox Sports

"Loved the book!! Can't wait for the next installment..."
- Larry Mainland, actor, *The Walking Dead, Lawless,
The Three Stooges*

"The action comes swift, and doesn't stop until the final pages. *Crossfire* tells a great story of betrayal and revenge."
- C.R. Blevins, writer, *A Western Tale*

"This was my first introduction to The Wraith and I was not disappointed. The action comes swift, and doesn't stop until the final pages.... If you love a good action/hero story, you will certainly enjoy reading *Crossfire.*"
- Ally, *Amazon*

"Makes me want more...should be the next series on Netflix..."
- Bill Lancaster, *Amazon*

"Another excellent entry in The Wraith Adventures series. Thoroughly recommended for Wraith fans and fans of pulp super-heroics."
- Leon Mallett, *Amazon*

Praise for *Cult of the Damned*

"Only by the first three pages, Frank Dirscherl wonderfully captures a dark and mysterious atmosphere, one that leaves the reader with a cryptic and eerie sensation; one that makes me cold just thinking about it."

> – Rennie Cowan, writer/director, *The Thriller Idol: A Tribute to the Legacy of Michael Jackson, Kade the Conqueror*

"Frank Dirscherl pulls you into the world of The Wraith from the first sentence and refuses to let you go until the last one."

> – Stephen J. Semones, writer/director, *Beyond the Lens, Crossfire, The Wraith: Eyes of Judgment*

"The Wraith is one of my favorite characters and every time Frank Dirscherl puts pen to paper I know I'm in for a real treat."

> – A.P. Fuchs, writer, *The Axiom-man Saga, The Way of the Fog, Undead World trilogy*

Praise for *Cry of the Werewolf*

"Frank Dirscherl delivers beyond measure.... The solid characters, settings and story really propel you page to page and leave you hanging on for more."
- Stephen J. Semones, writer/director, *Beyond the Lens, Crossfire, The Wraith: Eyes of Judgment*

"Each new installment in *The Wraith Adventures* series is a guaranteed good time filled with high adventure, romance and pulpy fun. Dirscherl is at the top of his form."
- A.P. Fuchs, writer, *The Axiom-man Saga, The Way of the Fog, Undead World trilogy*

"The writing is well done and well edited, and is filled with that distinct Dirscherl style of pulp that I enjoy so much. The book is a perfect example of what Neo Pulp/Superhero and Horror fiction can be and is a worthy addition to any fan's collection."
- Marcus Bucklin, *Amazon*

Praise for *Vendetta*

"...in all a great brew that had me hooked for the whole ride. Now bring on the next book, Frank..."

– Leon Mallett, Amazon

"This book starts with a literal bang and doesn't let the foot off of the gas until the very last page. The book is well plotted and moves at a breakneck pace, making it an enjoyable, short read. I loved this book very much as a fan of The Wraith and I believe that anyone who is a fan of the series should consider this required reading."

– Marcus Bucklin, Amazon

Praise for *Werewolves Attack!* in *Metahumans vs Werewolves*

BY FRANK DIRSCHERL

FICTION

The Wraith Dread Avenger of the Underworld series

1. *The Wraith*
2. *Valley of Evil*
3. *Crossfire* (with Stephen J. Semones)
4. *Cult of the Damned*
5. *Cry of the Werewolf*
6. *Swamp Witch of Satan's Forest* (with Ray MacKay)
7. *Vendetta*
8. *Lady Wraith* (with Adam Oravec)
9. *Kingdom*
10. *City of Fear*
11. *Birds of the Living Dead* - COMING SOON

12. *The Acolyte* - COMING SOON

Books of Judgment sub-series

1. *Sanderson of Metro* (with Bobby Nash)
2. *Serpent Rising* (with Greg Gick)
3. *Rising Son* (with Adam Oravec) - COMING SOON

SHORT STORY COLLECTIONS

Metahumans vs. Robots
Metahumans vs. the Ultimate Evil
The Wraith Vol. 1
The Wraith Vol. 2 - COMING SOON
Lance Star – Sky Ranger Vol. 1

NON-FICTION

The Wraith: Eyes of Judgment – The Official Script Book & Movie Guide (with Stephen J. Semones)
The Hitchers of Oz
Beyond the Lens (edited)

www.glowingeyesmedia.com

CITY OF FEAR

The Wraith Dread Avenger of the Underworld #10

by

Frank Dirscherl

GLOWING EYES MEDIA

WOLLONGONG

GLOWING EYES MEDIA
PO Box 31
Wollongong NSW 2520

ISBN 978-0-646-72133-0

CITY OF FEAR

PUBLISHED BY GLOWING EYES MEDIA, August 2025
www.glowingeyesmedia.com
FRONT COVER ART by Anon
COVER LAYOUT AND DESIGN AND INTERIOR DESIGN by Frank Dirscherl
EDITED by AP Fuchs and Joanne Lane at FirstEditing.com
FIRST EDITION

For more on *City of Fear*
visit www.glowingeyesmedia.com

Text set in Garamond-Normal. Printed and bound in the USA

A catalogue record for this book is available from the National Library of Australia

The Wraith Dread Avenger of the Underworld series in correct reading order (including short stories)

So far...but the story goes on...

This one is for my longtime Wraith fans...hope this is a suitable payoff for you

CITY OF FEAR

~ Prologue ~

SEVERAL YEARS AGO

The airship sped onward, up through the clouds, causing Natalya Blackova to rely on her instruments to navigate the craft. It was a cloudy night, with storms forecast to barrel down upon Metro city on the morrow. Magnus Khan sat in the chair beside Blackova, while the Cobra stared out the window.

Just then, The Wraith burst into the cockpit. Khan was the first to meet him.

"Time for round two," The Wraith said.

Khan growled as he began the battle, and while The Wraith's strength had been diluted, his anger, his determination, was stronger than ever before. Where Khan had been close to his physical equal in their previous encounter, his anger now knew no bounds. Evading each of Khan's blows, The Wraith lashed out, ending the battle with one powerful strike.

Blackova dared not react, for the craft had just experienced some slight turbulence and needed her full attention. Her master was on his own.

"Abdelkrim!" The Wraith boomed. "You will not escape me again. I have not forgotten your atrocities in Africa."

The Cobra growled with fury, and they battled there, in the cramped zeppelin cockpit, not only for their lives but the lives of everyone in Metro City. The struggle was fierce, with neither quarry gaining any advantage. Blows of inconceivable force were blocked and traded. There wasn't much room to evade them, and both combatants were soon showing the evidence of their battle. The Cobra finally lashed out with a strong uppercut, which slammed The Wraith into the wall opposite. Blood was splattered on the faces of both warriors, as they paused briefly, eyeing each other off.

"It is fitting to finish this here, above your beloved city," the Cobra said slowly. "We are the only two worthy to hold her in his hands." Then, as if in afterthought, he added, "After our previous encounters, and what you did to me, it is indeed fitting to fight for her here in the stratosphere."

The Wraith wiped the blood from his nose and stepped forward. "You let others fight your battles and flee like the coward you are. I did nothing to you. You *are* nothing! Metro City will never be yours."

"Then let us finish this now."

The Cobra launched himself at The Wraith, whose speed now failed him, and slammed into him, sending them both careening into the far wall. The Wraith grunted in pain as the Cobra reached for his throat, attempting to squeeze the life from him.

"You gave me this power I have," the Cobra snarled. "It was my destiny to receive everything from the old man."

The Wraith reached up, trying to break free from the villain's iron grip. "You were not worthy then...you are still not worthy."

The Cobra, furious, pulled him forward, never lessening his grip on his throat. He slammed The Wraith back into the wall repeatedly until he was close to unconsciousness. The Cobra did so for a fourth time, but this time the wall failed to hold under the incredible force smashing into it.

The Wraith and the Cobra plummeted out into the cold night, falling to their potential doom.

As they plunged through the icy air, The Wraith knew there was no hope of using his cloak to float to safety, not at this velocity. The only hope of survival was if he reached out for the ladder before it was too late. He had to move–*now!* Using his left arm–the stronger of the two since injuring his right in the leap for the rope ladder earlier–he grabbed the last rung and screamed in pain as his shoulder dislocated from its socket. Somehow, his fingers held tight and firm. Seconds later, the Cobra whizzed down past him and, in one last desperate grab for survival, latched on to The Wraith's ankle. He screamed and couldn't hang on with the added burden of someone the size and weight of the Cobra for long. Before his hand gave way, he thrust his right hand up and gripped the rung. His left arm now dangled lifelessly by his side. He knew, even with his good arm, he couldn't hold for long under the load of two large, heavily muscled men.

The Wraith looked down and saw his adversary staring up at him. The Cobra peered up with mocking eyes, struggling to maintain his grip on his enemy's ankle. The Cobra then grinned, as if he knew fate had somehow dealt him a different hand.

"Did I not say it was fitting," the Cobra shouted above the noise of the wind and the airship's engine, "to end this here? Indeed, although it is not the end I anticipated."

As his words were drowned out by the stark winds, his grip on The Wraith's ankle faltered...

...and he fell.

He didn't scream.

The Wraith, his body battered and bruised, pulled himself up and gripped the ladder rung under his right elbow. At least he was safe...for the time being.

Suddenly, the airship began to swerve, as if trying to shake him off. The Wraith realized that one or both of the two in the cockpit knew the Cobra was lost and was trying to gain retribution by shaking him off. He held tight with his remaining strength, but it was tough with the swaying of the aircraft and the now high wind threatening to loosen him from his perch. As impossible as the situation seemed with his injuries, he had to make his way back up to the cockpit. Slowly but surely, as the airship buffeted in the storm, The Wraith struggled to the top. Finally, he staggered inside the cockpit, and saw Khan still lying prone on the floor.

Natalya Blackova remained at the helm of the airship, now rocking wildly, due both to the impact of the storm and to her mad attempts at revenge against The Wraith. The Wraith's mind reeled–what was he to do? He had to take control of the ship, but he knew it wouldn't be easy, and he barely had the strength to stand, let alone engage in another battle. Did she even know he had returned to the cockpit? Perhaps he could surprise her and end this with little effort.

Before he had a chance to conceive a plan of action, Blackova whirled and fired a high-powered pistol at him. "Die!"

The Wraith managed to evade the initial barrage, but the bullets kept coming, and one found its mark in his upper right thigh, shattering his femur. The Wraith shouted in anguish, retreated, slipping back through the large opening caused by his previous battle with the Cobra. He gained a firm hold at the top of the ladder. Gaining control of the ship and landing it safely was no longer an option, not in his physical condition, and staying aboard the cockpit was clearly impossible. As it was, he could hardly consider what course of action to take next; his pain was indescribable.

No sooner had he lamented the current situation, the zeppelin banked downward sharply. He could barely hang on. The airship careened down through the clouds and the burrough of Gladstone's skyline quickly became visible.

The Wraith was helpless as Blackova madly banked the ship, aiming for the nearest tall building. His mind raced.

Is she so insane with rage as to sacrifice her life in order to get her revenge on me?

The Wraith dangled there, his left shoulder badly torn from its socket, his right shoulder strained to the limit, blood flowing from wounds to the face and thigh. He tried to gather his thoughts. It couldn't end this way. To have defeated the greatest evil he had ever known, only for his own end to come so soon after victory.

No, not now.

With the ship dangerously close to the building, it banked upward sharply, sending the rope ladder toward the building at great speed. The Wraith knew there was only one hope and a slim one perhaps. Sliding down the ladder as far he could, he prepared himself. Seeing a window close by, he let go of the ladder and crashed through it, and a desk behind it, before smashing into the wall at the far end of the empty office.

He lay there, finally able to rest. He'd survived. Somehow. Unconsciousness beckoned, and in the seconds he had remaining he knew it had been worth it despite what he'd been through. The Cobra had been defeated and a great pall had been lifted from the city. To save his city, to rescue innocents, he would sacrifice all, even his life, in his endless war against evil. This day, he had survived, barely, and while some had escaped, the Cobra had perished in battle.

As these thoughts drifted through his mind, blackness enveloped him.

* * * * * *

LATER THAT NIGHT

Metro City truly came alive at night. By day, it was a bustling metropolis like so many others. Business people flocked here and there, from office to coffee shop and back, meeting place to meeting place. Shoppers scurried about the main streets, using the high fashion boutiques as a playground. But it was nighttime when the shadows slithered forth, engulfing all that was good in the city in its inky, wicked embrace, and giving the city its dreadful reputation. Evil latched on to the city and its people as soon as the sun set, and it was loath to loosen that grip come the following morning.

Down by the dilapidated Christopher Docks in the now largely disused historic waterfront district (long since replaced by more modern facilities further along the coast), a dense fog billowed and rolled in from the Atlantic. Horns blared, the sound of waves slapped against the wharf pylons and a few small ships moored there bobbed up and down in the darkness as a large human form emerged from the water with a burst of froth and bubbles.

The lumbering form clambered up onto the rickety wooden structure, his weight causing the dock to moan and creak in abject protest. Collecting himself, heaving the air back into his lungs, he slowly trudged through the haze, marching silently out toward the abandoned warehouses.

Entering a dark alley, he rounded a corner and entered another, one of an infinite number located in that part of the city. The figure passed a series of homeless people and hookers plying their filthy trade in the nooks and crannies of this area referred to as Hell on Earth.

As the hulking figure continued his lonesome journey, a drunk stumbled from a seedy bar and practically slammed into him. The drunk rubbed his eyes in a vain attempt to see more clearly.

"Aye, ye a big lad, ain't ye?" the drunk slurred.

The figure remained silent and continued his slow march down the alley. He passed the short, portly drunken man, unshaven and dressed in clothing that had seen better days, ignoring him completely.

"Aye!" the drunk said sharply. "Are ye deaf? I'm talking with ye, man."

The figure continued to disregard the drunk who struggled to catch up and finally grabbed his cape in an attempt to whirl him around. The drunk fell to the ground in the attempt.

"Ufff...ye bast..." he grunted as he labored to his feet.

The drunk stopped in his tracks, as the figure now focused his attention fully on him. Coming into the light of a nearby street lamp, the figure's facial features became apparent. A large, cobra-shaped scar–or tattoo–surrounded his right eye, which was a horrendous milky white. Shoulder-length jet-black hair surrounded a powerful, cruel face. He was wearing a red and black outfit, form-fitting and armored with metallic, golden serpents completing the look.

"Fool!" the figure boomed. "Do you not know who I am? Do you not know that I am to be master of this city?"

The terrified drunk struggled in a vain attempt to backtrack and flee. In doing so, he crashed against some nearby trash cans, and fell in a sloppy heap into the putrid puddle.

"The Wraith took much from me," the figure continued. "But his end will come. My destiny has been foretold. Nothing will stop me. Nothing will stop–"

The figure reached down and yanked the hapless drunk into the air with one powerful arm. He pulled the drunk in close.

"–the Cobra!"

The Cobra's right eye began to glow and crackle with an ethereal energy.

The drunk screamed.

* * * * * *

THE PRESENT

Paul Sanderson and Leena Patterson closed Emily's bedroom door softly behind them.

"She's such a doll," Leena said. "So sweet."

"She's been through Hell and back," Paul said. "I hope she can heal here and learn to love and trust again."

"She will, darling. She will."

Jonathan Simpson, the household butler, hovered nearby. "Will Miss Emily be requiring dinner, sir?"

"I'm not sure, Simpson," he replied. "I doubt it, but remain on standby for a while, in case she wakes up early."

"I will make a little something that can be easily re-heated later, perhaps."

"Good idea," Leena said.

The butler retreated down the hallway of the Sanderson House mansion. Paul and Leena slowly followed suit.

"Instant parenthood is such a big change to our lives," Leena said. "I hope we're ready."

"We're as ready as we'll ever be," Paul said as they reached the grand staircase leading downstairs. "Can anyone ever truly be ready for such a monumental occurrence in their lives?"

Leena seemed to agree with that sentiment.

"Love will win out, as it always does. As it always must," Paul said.

Simpson greeted them at the foot of the stairs, a look of grave concern etched into his hardened features.

"Simpson, what's wrong?" Leena said.

"Master Max," the butler said, "he sounds...not well."

"Max? Ill?" Paul said. He knew full well Max had never been sick a day in his life. He had the fortitude of an ox. "He seemed fine earlier. Where is he?"

"In the Lair, sir," Simpson said. "He said he needs your help immediately."

It sounded serious. Paul looked at Leena, who immediately nodded in return. Without another thought, they both headed toward the library. Paul reached the desk first, opened a drawer, and removed a small remote control device. Pressing the button caused a small section of the adjacent bookcase to slide open with a whooshing of gears. An instant later, they were inside, descending in the small, oval elevator. Max stood sentinel-like beside the Lair's computer terminal. The back of the chair faced Paul and Leena.

"Max, is everything okay?" Paul said, noticing his friend was as rigid and emotionless as a statue. He was pale and unresponsive.

"You look terrible," Leena added. "You better come upstairs and get some rest. Maybe..."

"My master has been waiting for you," Max finally said in monotone fashion.

"Master?" Leena said. "What on Earth are you talking about?"

"He is referring to me," a deep voice emanated throughout the Lair.

It was a voice Paul was familiar with. He hadn't heard it for years, but it was something he could never forget. For the first time in years, he was truly frightened.

The chair beside Max pivoted to reveal the Cobra, alive and well as they had feared. His milky right eye shone and his smile revealed a cruelty rarely seen in any human being.

"I have returned," the Cobra said with some menace. "Welcome me home."

~ Chapter 1 ~

"**A**bdelkrim," Paul breathed, trying valiantly to hide his great apprehension, but sure he was failing. 1

"How gratifying," the Cobra said, his unholy smile never leaving his face, a slight tinge of gray in his temples. "You remember me. How appropriate, for I have never forgotten you, or what you have taken from me."

"What are you talking about?" Leena said in a raised voice, her emotions clearly getting the better of her.

The Cobra raised a finger. "Silence, wench!" His right eye sparkled.

Paul was shocked to find Leena frozen in position. He reached over to shake her free from the spell, but she felt as stiff as a board and as cold as death.

What power!

Sweat began to form on Paul's brow. His mind raced with the seriousness of the situation. But there were no immediate answers to his current nightmare. He was utterly in the Cobra's grasp.

"What have you done with her?" Paul demanded.

The Cobra evidently took great pleasure in his ascendancy. "She is unharmed. I have only silenced her...for now." He shifted in his seat. "You stole my woman, so is it not fitting if I was to take yours?" The menace, the implicit threat in his voice, was abundantly clear.

Woman? Paul thought. *Natalya Blackova? Of course, he still thinks she perished all those years ago. He's completely unaware of what has occurred in the years since.* 2

"You will never have her," Paul said in defiance.

"Strong words," the Cobra mocked, "but you are in no position for such bravado." He stood. "You still do not realize the peril you are in, do you? The danger you now face."

"Oh, I think I have an idea," Paul said.

The Cobra smirked. "Really? Well, as you are no threat to me, allow me to reveal a few interesting pieces of information that I am sure you have not yet fully comprehended."

As the Cobra spoke, pacing left and right, Max remained in position, as though he were made of stone and not flesh and blood.

In that moment, the upstairs entry to the Lair opened with a whirring of gears, and the butler Simpson appeared on the upper landing. "Master Paul, sir, does Master Max require any assistance?"

Paul had no time to react. The Cobra was swift and merciless.

"Lackey," the Cobra boomed. "You dare interrupt this conference of your superiors?"

Paul knew what was coming. "Abdelkrim, no!"

"Silence!" the Cobra moaned, and Paul, too, became instantly immobile. His free will remained, but he was completely incapable of speech or movement.

The Cobra has so much power now, Paul thought as he tried valiantly to break free from his bonds. But it was as though his brain was inexplicably disconnected from his body. Apart from the blinking of his eyes, the beating of his heart, and the movement of his lungs expanding within his chest, he was incapable of anything else. He was absolutely helpless.

"Lackey!" the Cobra said again, returning his attention to Simpson. "You will do anything to please me."

Simpson stood bolt upright, no longer in control of his body. "Yes, master."

"Step forth, and prove your devotion, your undying devotion, to the Cobra."

Simpson did as commanded. Without any hesitation, without any sign of doubt or sensation, the butler walked over to the section of the platform where the elevator would ordinarily be. He stepped over the edge, into nothingness, and plummeted to the floor in a horrifying display of the Cobra's callous, remorseless power.

Paul screamed silently, watching Simpson's body smacking into the hard floor of the Lair with a sickening crack. He feared the worst. And he could do nothing about it.

"As I deal with all who get in my way," the Cobra said, a lascivious smile curling upon his lips. "Now, to return to matters of greater importance...you must wonder how I come to be alive. Well, it is no great mystery. A being as powerful as myself could not possibly perish after a mere fall into a body of water."

Paul continued to struggle with all his strength, though it did not show at all. The battle for control of his body lay within, but he was unable to break free from the Cobra's incredible will.

"After resurfacing, I have been here, within your city, refocusing, rebuilding my strength for the battle that lay ahead. I admit you were a more formidable foe than I had initially anticipated. So, I waited. I meditated. And I watched. I watched as you murdered my beloved Natalya. I witnessed your incarceration of my dearly departed servant, Magnus Khan."

Khan; there's a name I haven't heard in ages. So, it was *the Cobra that assassinated him.* 3

"I have bided my time and amassed my strength and forces to take what is rightfully mine; a destiny that was stolen from me. But no longer." The Cobra nodded toward Paul, who suddenly felt the muscles of his throat and face relax.

"You've been here...all these years?" Paul asked, incredulous. He could speak once again, but still could not move.

"Of course," the Cobra said. "Do you still not understand?" He cackled briefly, an extremely disconcerting sight and sound. "Have you not noticed a feeling of dread, a downcast sensation within this city for quite some time?" The Cobra paused for a moment. "I see from your expression that you are finally beginning to grasp the situation. Yes, that was me. I have slowly been exerting control upon the people of this city for years. As my power increased, so did my level of control. Your city has now become my city, as it was always meant to be. My destiny has long been foretold, and my plans are finally coming to fruition." 4

A nauseousness began to almost overwhelm Paul, but he managed to hold it together. The realization of everything being revealed to him was almost too much to bear. And Simpson, poor Simpson.

"How long has Max been in your power?"

The Cobra briefly appeared confused, then recognized whom Paul was referring to on his right. "This infidel? Oh, I believe it was while you were away on vacation. That is how the locals would put it, is it not?"

While we were away in the mountains, dealing with Satanish and his army of werewolves. 5

"But enough of my prattling," the Cobra said after a few moments. He strode toward Paul's still inert form. "I have what I came for." He now stood directly before his great adversary.

"And what is that?" Paul said.

"I have shown you that you are completely powerless to stop me. You truly are the gnat I always knew you to be. For taking my Natalya from me and delaying my destiny, you will pay. Pay dearly. I will take everything from you. Everything you hold dear. And then, when you are broken, defiled, ready to beg me for mercy, I will peel the flesh from your bones! And I will rule for all time!"

The Cobra's eyes narrowed, his face crueler and more malevolent than ever before. The villain retreated back a few steps, raised a hand and then...

Darkness.

* * * * * *

Paul gasped as though bursting from a raging torrent, his lungs expanding with long sought after air, only he hadn't been drowning and there was no torrent.

He fell to his knees, weak, still trying to hack the air back into his lungs. Only after a further few moments did he finally come to his senses and realize he was free once again.

He sprang to his feet, adrenaline flooding his limbs and ready and willing to battle the Cobra there and then. But the villain was gone, and there was no sign of him or of Max. Paul checked his Erebus Ascent wristwatch. It was almost 9:00 AM the following morning. Suddenly he felt overwhelmed and found it difficult to make sense of everything. His brain was foggy, unfocused.

"Paul?"

He turned quickly and saw Leena standing there, finally coming to herself and clearly confused. He took her in his arms. "Darling, you're all right."

"What...what just happened?" she asked.

Then it finally hit him. Simpson. He hadn't a moment to lose. "Quickly," he said, and rushed over to where his butler lay.

Leena followed and gasped at the sight of the old man. Paul crouched down and felt for a pulse. It was extremely weak, but still evident. From his position on the floor, Paul felt certain the butler had broken his neck, and he dared not move him.

"Is he...he...?"

"He needs urgent medical attention," Paul said.

"But...here in the Lair?"

Paul thought for a moment and looked about him. "We'll need to secure his neck first. In the MediLab over there, find a neck brace and bring it over here."

Leena raced over to their fully equipped medical facility, rifled through a few drawers, and found what she was looking for. She returned an instant later.

"Good work," Paul said. "Now, help me get this around his neck as carefully as possible."

Leena held Simpson as still as she could while Paul slipped the brace into position. The first aid course he had recently completed was certainly paying off.

"Now, bring that gurney there over here and we'll carry the poor fellow out into the grounds and call an ambulance," Paul said.

Again, Leena did as directed, and they carried their dear friend out toward the tunnel connecting the Lair to the home's garage. Soon they were standing in the estate's driveway.

"I'll head back inside and call for an ambulance," Leena said, already starting back for the garage.

"Wait," Paul said. "We have only a short time to get this right. We have to position poor Simpson in just the right place, beneath a window, and disturb the ground beneath him, so as not to arouse any suspicion. We can't afford any questions to be asked."

"But that would look like–"

"We'll deal with that later; we haven't time for anything else. Quickly now."

And with that, Leena was off.

~ Chapter 2 ~

"**M**mm."

Emily awoke with a yawn and a stretch of her arms. She slowly sat upright and rubbed her eyes. Finally, she relented and opened them. 6

"Oh," she said, at the sight of Paul seated in the chair by her bed. She showed no sign of fear or surprise, and she smiled at the sight of him. "What time is it?"

"After ten," Paul replied, looking at his watch. "You've been asleep a long time."

"This bed is comfy," Emily said, stretching her arms once again.

"You must be starving," he said. "Are you ready for breakfast?"

The little girl rubbed her tummy. "Yes, please."

"Well then," Paul said, standing, "do you like pancakes? I don't mean to brag, but I'm famous for making the best pancakes in town."

"I love pancakes!" she squealed.

"Then come on," Paul said, "and I'll treat you with as many pancakes as you like."

Emily leaped out of bed and launched herself into Paul's arms, giving him the hug of a lifetime. "Thank you for looking after me and giving me this wonderful new home. I feel so happy."

Tears of joy welled in Paul's eyes. His heart swelled with love for the beautiful little girl in his arms. She and Leena were really all he needed. "Me too," he finally replied. "Me too."

As they walked, hand-in-hand, out into the hallway and down the grand staircase, Paul knew it was important not to let their troubles and struggles seep into her life. Emily had been through so much already. All he wanted for her was a life of joy, fun, and love.

When they reached the breakfast room, they found Leena already seated there in the nook with a smile on her face. She was keeping up the charade that all was well.

"There you both are," Leena said. "I was wondering if we'd ever start breakfast."

"I'm sorry I kept you," Emily said, appearing chagrined.

Paul smiled broadly and bent down to the little girl. "Not at all. We're just happy you got a good night's rest. You clearly needed it."

She grinned a big toothy grin, no longer upset or embarrassed.

"Now, you just take a seat over there and let me get to work on those pancakes."

As Paul started in the adjacent kitchen, Emily sat alongside Leena and got comfortable. Paul peeped over at his new family occasionally, and noticed that his little girl was chatting amiably with Leena and taking delight in the delicious meal to come.

Later, when the three of them were seated, they devoured a giant platter of pancakes, talking, laughing, and thoroughly enjoying each other's company. At last, after having her fill, Emily looked up, her face covered with syrup and jam.

"Where is the other man?" she said, licking her lips.

Leena raised an eyebrow at Paul, who answered, "Oh, umm...Simpson became ill last night. He had to take a trip to the hospital just to see that he's all right."

"Oh no, poor man," Emily said, her face clouding over with sadness. "Mommy said my daddy was taken to hospital when I was little. He never came back."

Paul stood and moved over to the little girl's side, crouching down. "Simpson will be okay, honey, I promise you. He just needs some medicine and he'll be home soon, okay?"

She smiled, seemed mollified by that. "Okay."

"Now," Paul said. "Let's get you cleaned up first. Would you like to play in the garden after that?"

* * * * * *

Detective Bob Sloan strode into the main squad room with a spring in his step. He whistled, acknowledged his colleagues with a nod, and made his way over to his desk. His partner, Detective Rosa Perez, a pretty but plain young Latina, was already seated at her desk next to his.

"You're in early," Sloan said as he plopped into his chair.

"No, you're late," Perez said, with a glint in her eye.

Sloan looked down at his battered Timex watch. "Hmm...later than I thought."

"Uh huh," Perez said. "After everything we've–*you've*–been through, you clearly needed the rest." 7

Sloan lifted his baseball cap from his head and put a hand through his thinning locks. "Maybe."

Perez chuckled. "C'mon, Bob, admit it. You're tired. Look at all the crap we've been through, and this city has been through."

"Okay, okay, I had a nice lie in," Sloan finally admitted. "So, sue me."

"It's a good thing. You bloody well needed it."

Sloan knew the truth of her words.

"I just had a thought...I had a break recently. Maybe it's time you did, too. When was the last time you had a vacation with Janet? Have you ever had one?"

"Hey there, you're ruining my good mood," Sloan said. "I got a bit of extra rest, true, and I did need that, but a vacation?"

"Yes, Bob. You know what a vacation is, right? Normal people have them all the time, or at least semi-regularly."

Sloan frowned at his partner. "Gimme a break, Perez."

"At least mull it over, okay?" Perez said. "My time away did me the world of good. Surely you could do with some downtime. You must have years of leave built up."

Sloan gave it a moment's thought. It wasn't a bad idea. He'd been a workaholic for years. His entire working life, actually. His wife Janet had put up with it and long since accepted it. Maybe it was time to devote some of his energies to his family. Maybe they could go to an island somewhere and do some sunbathing, fishing, and eat good food.

"Bob?"

Sloan was brought back to reality. "I will think about it, Perez, I promise. In the meantime, I have some overdue reports to complete before Harrison fires my ass. Then we can finally put that pandemic issue to bed."

Sloan saw Perez's lips tighten, and she hunched down over her desk and got back to work. He smiled. He appreciated her thinking of his wellbeing, but he still had a job to do, and he set about doing so.

* * * * * *

The Cobra sat cross-legged atop a large plush oriental cushion on the floor; his eyes closed in intense concentration and his arms raised in front of him. He was positioned at the far end of a cavernous, lavishly decorated room filled with decorations and ornaments from a variety of cultures–Iranian, Eritrean, Ethiopian, and a host of others. Max Horton stood in silence, sentinel-like by his master's side.

This went on for minutes, then hours. During this time, both the Cobra and Max remained completely still, neither moving the merest inch. Then, the Cobra's eyebrows began to twitch, slowly at first, then faster. Then his eyes started rolling beneath his still-shut eyelids. And then his entire body began to vibrate. He began to hum in a rhythmic fashion. Building in intensity, it concluded in a crescendo of movement and noise.

The Cobra's eyes snapped open. All noise and movement ceased. "It is done. My people are primed." He stood and remained focused on nothing and everything all at once, before finally turning to the only other person in the room. "Has the construction commenced?"

Max came to life at this, to a fashion, replying in a monotone manner. "Yes, master. I have seen to it personally. The sphere will be a large one, just as you commanded."

"Excellent," the Cobra said, allowing himself a hint of self-satisfaction. "Shipment of the sphere's contents will be received soon." He began to pace before his bewitched lackey. "And, to ensure nothing prevents delivery of said shipment, I have prepared my people to act accordingly."

At this, Blackstorm, one of the Cobra's many-thus named warriors, entered, and paid his master homage. Blackstorm was outfitted as his brethren in gray tactical armor that covered him from head to foot. A red cobra was emblazoned on his upper left chest. A mask akin to that of a hockey goalkeeper hid his identity. 8

"Yes, you may speak," the Cobra said.

"Your men are ready to do your bidding, master," Blackstorm said, his voice muffled.

"Their presence is not yet required," the Cobra said. "The people of this city will suffice for my purposes."

Blackstorm bowed and made to exit.

"However," the Cobra said, "perhaps surveillance is justified at this juncture." He rubbed his goatee. "Ascertain the whereabouts of The Wraith and his infidels at all times. Reconnaissance only at this point. My people will surely keep him busy enough to allow my destiny to be fulfilled. See to it personally. Now go!"

Blackstorm did not hesitate, exiting quickly and leaving the Cobra alone with Max once again.

"Nothing must delay my destiny any longer. This city must fall!"

~ Chapter 3 ~

The computer terminal hummed with a fervent, electrical sensation. It was the only audible sound within the expansive Lair structure, located in the center of the Sanderson House mansion. Paul, outfitted as The Wraith but sans cowl, sat at the terminal, hunched over, his chin in his hands, deep in thought.

Max, my friend, kidnapped and brainwashed, The Wraith ruminated. *My headquarters compromised, my secrets potentially at peril. My family at risk. This city...Metro...*

It was all too much to bear. He pondered if he had reached his lowest ebb. He had never been as helpless or lost as he was now, and he was at a loss about his next move. The Cobra currently held all the cards. And, therefore, the next move, by necessity, had to be his enemy's. It galled him no end that the Cobra now appeared more powerful and formidable than ever. Anger, frustration, terror, sorrow. All these raw emotions and more rolled around in his brain, beating at him like a hammer.

"There you are," Leena's voice came through from the Lair's upper landing.

"I didn't know where else to go," Paul said.

Leena descended in the compact elevator. In moments, she stood beside him. "You're in your uniform. I assume you intend undertaking your regular patrol?"

He swiveled in his chair to face his fiancée. "I need to do more. Max needs our help. We can't let the Cobra remain at large. Whatever he has planned, undoubtedly all life is at stake." He slammed a fist into one of his chair's armrests. "And that villain has the upper hand."

"You're right," she said in a soothing tone, "but we're not as helpless as you might think."

He looked at her, wondering what she had in mind.

"Think about it. Somebody must know something. Remember the recent human trafficking ring you broke? Troy Bramson was clearly working for the Cobra. That had to be why he was silenced. He knew too much. There must be others like him. Somebody *must* know something."

He knew she was right, inwardly chided himself for wallowing in self-pity, especially now in the hour of the greatest need. He couldn't let the Cobra triumph. And he sure as hell wouldn't let his friend Max down. Leena had shamed him into action.

"Let me suit up and we'll be on our way," Leena said, heading swiftly to the rack of uniforms that adorned the far wall.

"I think I know who we'll visit first," Paul said.

* * * * * *

The Wraith and Lady Wraith stood majestically atop the Latham Industries building, peering out at the glistening city skyline. From their vantage point, Metro looked so beautiful, pristine, and pure. How ironic that the city was anything but. Nevertheless, it was filled with his people, both good and bad. And they all deserved to live their lives.

"You think he'll show up?" The Wraith said at last.

"I don't doubt it," Lady Wraith said.

The Wraith checked his Héron Marinor wristwatch. "We'd better head down there."

Both pulled a grapnel device from their respective belts and used them to repel down into the street. They slid down effortlessly and landed on the street with a soft thud. The Wraith activated his night-vision lenses, and they quickly darted into a side alley. It was deserted.

"Where is he?" Lady Wraith asked quietly.

Before The Wraith could answer, they were interrupted by the sound of a ruckus coming from the main thoroughfare behind them. Curious, The Wraith sidled to the corner and peered out into the street. What he saw and heard there astonished him. A growing crowd of people were fighting each other. Lady Wraith joined him to bear witness to this strange phenomenon. What surely had started as a minor scuffle now escalated before their very eyes into a major battle.

"What the...?!" Lady Wraith said.

A crowd of people assaulted each other in the most violent fashion. Punching, wrestling, biting, with more men and women–quite clearly from all corners of life–joining in from adjoining buildings and parked cars. There was no rhyme or reason to it. No one tried to calm the situation, and no one attempted to do anything other than join in. As the two watched on with sickening fascination, the crowd grew larger and larger, and the violence evermore potent.

"We have to stop this," The Wraith finally said, utterly confused by all he was seeing.

He plunged out into the street before Lady Wraith had any chance to respond.

"People!" he cried out, trying to reach to the crowd above the din. "You must stop this!"

They completely ignored him. He wondered if they had even noticed his presence.

"They're mad," Lady Wraith said, obviously flustered. "Uncontrollable."

"Quickly, before the crowd grows even more," The Wraith said, reaching into his belt.

He raced toward the riot and lobbed several gas pellets at various parts of the group. A thick, pungent smoke erupted at their feet, and The Wraith and Lady Wraith wasted no time, taking advantage of this brief respite, diving in amongst them, feet and fists flailing.

"Take as many down as you can," The Wraith shouted. "We must prevail."

He launched himself at all and sundry with a savage fury. The Wraith didn't know why these people were behaving in such a bizarre and ferocious fashion, but there was clearly no reasoning with them, and the only answer that proved effective was further hostility. He lashed out with powerful rights and lefts, undercuts, and muscular blows to the stomach. He could hear Lady Wraith making similar short work with her adversaries behind him, and he continued the battle.

After some minutes, the haze started to lift, and it was evident there were still plenty of people lingering, insanity flashing in their eyes, their sole intent to maim and kill. The ferocity they exhibited was truly alarming. The Wraith had never seen such raw fury in so many people at once. He could make no sense of it.

As he dealt with each one, he glanced briefly at his partner, who was dealing with a series of attackers of her own.

"There's too many of them," Lady Wraith cried out. "I dare not use my Eyes of Judgment."

The Wraith knew she was referring to Max's unique invention. The combination of high-powered LED lights with Max's patented flash powder could either temporarily blind an opponent or obliterate them, depending on which function was chosen. The latter was, obviously, not an option, while the blinding feature could only work for a limited time in their current circumstances.

"We must retreat," The Wraith yelled. "There *are* too many of them, and more are joining in." He beckoned down the street, where even more people were heading toward them at speed, appearing as rabid as everyone else that night.

Positioned in the middle of the street, their options for flight were limited. An ever-building army of madmen surrounded them both, eager to tear them limb-from-limb.

"Use your blinding stare!" The Wraith screamed, practically overrun by assailants.

Suddenly, a blinding flash emanated from his rear, and a group of men cried out, stunned by the brightness of Lady Wraith's weapon. The advantage wouldn't hold long, so The Wraith did not tarry long. He barged through his group of attackers, grabbed Lady Wraith's arm, and broke free from the swarm. They sprinted for the nearest alley. Already he could hear the group quickly following them, baying for blood.

Upon reaching the alley, both swiftly aimed their grapnel guns skyward and were almost instantly yanked up into the night sky to safety.

Moments later, they stood on the rooftop of the building adjacent to the Latham corporate headquarters, trying to catch their breath.

"What was that all about?" Lady Wraith said, panting.

"I don't know," he said. "This is a nightmare."

"What in Heaven's name do we do?" she said, sounding almost desolate.

"We call this in," The Wraith said. "Sloan needs to know, the authorities need to prepare for the worst."

Lady Wraith's mouth dropped open, perhaps realizing the truth of the matter.

"Yes," The Wraith said in response. "I don't know how, but this is the Cobra's doing. Whatever else he may be planning, this is *his* doing. But why? Why?"

Frustration was near boiling point within him. Once again, the Cobra had the upper hand. The villain was toying with them, as a puppeteer would a marionette. And he was tired of feeling helpless.

Finally, he said, "I'll let Sloan know, then we'll work out our next step."

* * * * * *

The Cobra stood proudly in his monitor room that adjoined the throne room of his expansive hideaway. He had spent several years building this bolt hole right in the heart of his enemy's territory without The Wraith knowing. That reality always brought a special joy to his heart. In that time, he had amassed his strength and mental abilities in ways that even he had never thought possible. Now, he knew himself to truly be the most powerful in the world. With the merest thought, he could control any man, even groups of men, to do his bidding willingly, without hesitation.

And now, watching the various city news services on the monitors before him, he bore witness to the fruits of his incredible power. He was in control of large portions of the city's people–*his* people–and they were doing exactly as he wished. Soon, he would direct more of these sheep to follow suit, violently tearing each other apart in his name. Eventually, the entire city would be engulfed in such violence Metro City had never encountered before. All this was designed to keep his great nemesis occupied. And it was only the beginning.

"Master," Blackstorm said, striding into the room.

"I did not wish to be disturbed!" the Cobra said, raising his finger.

Blackstorm gasped, coughed, and reached up to his throat as though he was choking. After a few moments, the Cobra relented.

"M–master..." Blackstorm hacked. "I only bring word from one of our brethren."

The Cobra seemed almost disinterested; his attention focused solely on the carnage on view before him. "Yes," he said at last.

"Phase one of your operation has commenced," Blackstorm said. "The Wraith and Lady Wraith have met this initial onslaught and been found wanting."

That roused the Cobra from his reverie. "How so?"

"They resisted intensely but the odds overwhelmed them."

The Cobra allowed himself a brief cackle. "Ha! My great enemy disappoints me. If he cannot prove superior against such sheep–in such small initial numbers–perhaps I have overestimated his abilities all these years." He rubbed his goatee and paced to and fro. "No. It would not do to allow hubris to cloud my judgment. Despite his setback, he remains a formidable foe. Proceed as planned."

Blackstorm nodded, then quickly turned and returned whence he came. The Cobra returned his attention to the news broadcasts, enjoying the butchery he had wrought.

~ Chapter 4 ~

Fatback sat alone in his seedy, darkened apartment. His abode was extremely untidy. Clothing and boxes littered the floor so much there was no sign of the cheap linoleum underneath. The furniture was cut-rate and threadbare. The scurrying of roaches and rats could be heard everywhere. The stench of rotting food came from the adjacent kitchen. Fatback sat on a wooden chair, shivering and nervous. 9

"You've come down in the world," Lady Wraith said.

"Waaah!" Fatback shrieked, fairly leaping from his chair.

"Where were you, Fatty?" Lady Wraith said.

"Don't call me that!" Fatback said, frowning and attempting to fight back against his fear. He wasn't overly successful. "How did you get in here?"

A light strobed on. It was The Wraith's Eyes of Judgment. He was standing to Lady Wraith's right. Fatback's face shone brightly in terror.

"Where were you, Fatty?" Lady Wraith repeated.

"I'm sorry, I'm sorry, all right," Fatback said. "I headed out and then ran into...well, I'm sure you already know what's going on out there."

"What's going on out there?" The Wraith asked sharply.

"I don't know," Fatback said, perhaps a little louder than he had intended. "People are tearing themselves apart. I don't know why. Nothing to do with me. I hightailed it back here." He flopped back into his chair.

The Wraith crouched down, right in the thug's face, the Eyes on his chest crackling a fierce, ethereal energy. "What do you know of the Cobra?"

"Shhhh," Fatback hissed. He looked about him, as though they were being watched, or listened to.

"Tell me," The Wraith said through clenched teeth, spittle splashing on Fatback's face.

"I don't know nothing, okay? Nothing!"

"I think you do," The Wraith pressed.

"The Wraith is getting angry, Fatty. You won't like him when he's angry," Lady Wraith said, stepping forward.

The Wraith snarled and gnashed his teeth in response. Fatback looked ready to soil himself. And, in fact, he did.

"Tell me!" The Wraith growled. He grabbed the hapless thug by the collar, yanking his dripping carcass upward.

"All right, lemme go, lemme go," Fatback said.

The Wraith dropped him like a sack of soggy cement. "Talk!" The Eyes shone a brilliant, sickening yellow.

Fatback crawled around on the dirty and messy floor like an oversized albino cockroach. Whether he was trying to get comfortable or was merely panicking, The Wraith couldn't tell.

"Word on the street is, someone calling themselves...that...has been hiding out somewhere in the financial district of Metro." His voice wavered.

"The Cobra is secreted around Wall Street without our knowledge?" The Wraith couldn't believe what he was hearing, even though he knew it to be true. "Where exactly?"

"I don't know his address," Fatback said in a snarky fashion. "I'm not his realtor."

The Wraith grumbled, yanked Fatback up again, and slammed him into the far wall, sending chips of it outward in an explosion of dust and debris. "Where *is* he?"

"I...don't know...I tell you," Fatback coughed. "All I heard was mention of...the Fisky Building."

The Wraith let go once again, and the hapless thug fell heavily to the floor amongst the flotsam. "The Fisky Building. Let's go."

The Wraith barged out of the apartment's front door with Lady Wraith in hot pursuit.

* * * * * *

Fatback sat on his haunches and rubbed at a sore spot on the back of his head. He lamented his soiled trousers. Damn those avengers. Damn them all to Hades. Then he started to laugh. It was a slight chuckle at first, then a full-on belly laugh. It stretched on for minutes before he finally started to calm himself.

Then he started to think about changing his clothes.

* * * * * *

"We need every available man!" Commissioner George Harrison screamed into the squad room.

Every cop there shot bolt upright, including Sloan and Perez.

"The city's going crazy with hundreds, maybe thousands, rioting in the streets and fighting each other like rabid animals," Harrison said.

"Uniformed division is already on the streets, but not faring well at last report," Perez said, moving alongside Harrison. "Tear gas is completely ineffective."

"What about tranquilizer guns?" Sloan asked.

"We don't have enough of those to have any sort of impact at all," Harrison replied. Then he turned to face Perez. "Casualties?"

"At least three officers last I heard," Perez said solemnly.

"I think we need the National Guard," Sloan said, joining the pair.

"The state division has already made their way back to base after the recent pandemic," Harrison said. "It'll take some time to re-mobilize them."

"The local NG team then," Sloan said.

"I've put the call in. They're on the way. SWAT as well." Harrison looked stressed beyond belief. His toupée was on crooked. "But it's not enough. We need everyone." He shifted in front of the two cops and shouted, "I repeat, *everyone!*"

Sloan looked at his partner. This sounded like an emergency on an almost unimaginable scale, like none they had ever encountered.

Everyone, including Harrison, ran down the lengthy hallway leading to the armory; Sloan, Perez, and Harrison side-by-side.

"What the hell is going on here?" Sloan said, not to anyone in particular.

"Another pandemic? Mass poisoning?" Perez said.

"I don't know," Harrison said, his voice rougher than usual, "but we're spread pretty thin right now, and the odds are stacked against us. I don't think we're gonna come out of this with our heads held high."

Perez gasped a little at this.

Sloan also knew what Harrison was getting at. "Shoot to kill?"

"I don't see any other option," Harrison said. "It's like the people of this city have become zombies, like on a TV show. Nothing seems to stop them."

As they entered the armory, Sloan nodded grimly. The thought of firing on innocent civilians pained him, but he wasn't about to let himself, his colleagues, or friends be torn apart by an insane mob. Sadly, extreme measures were now clearly warranted, and he would take them to restore the peace. He only hoped he could live with himself afterward.

Harrison pulled a variety of pump action shotguns and AR-15 assault rifles from their secure positions along the wall, and handed them out to each officer. Each then retrieved a swag of ammunition and exited as quickly as they could.

"Which one?" Harrison said to Sloan. He and Perez were the last in the queue.

"Both," Sloan said.

Harrison seemed about to question that, but caught himself, nodded and gave Sloan the deadly weapons. Perez took a shotgun.

Now heavily armed, Sloan and Perez made for the exit. Sloan turned to see Harrison following suit, also armed to the hilt.

"Hey," Sloan said, "we can–"

"I said every available man," Harrison said. "And I meant it. I'm heading out with you two."

Sloan said nothing more and, before too long, the three of them were in Sloan's beat-up Buick, cruising the streets.

"Seems pretty quiet so far," Perez said, as they drove through the first couple of blocks surrounding Metro Police Plaza. "Not a soul about. That alone seems odd."

As they made a right into East 52nd Street, they realized they had spoken too soon. Up ahead of them was a large mass of people. As they neared, the situation became clearer and grimmer. Untold people were fighting amongst themselves in a fury Sloan had never seen before. Rabid was an understatement. Not even animals would behave in such a ferocious manner. It was almost as if everyone was possessed, bewitched somehow. No other description even came close to matching what they saw before them.

"Quickly," Harrison said, jumping from the vehicle.

"Sir, there's too many of them," Perez said, nevertheless following the commissioner's actions in exiting the car.

Sloan did likewise, and they retrieved their weapons from the car's trunk. It wasn't a moment too soon, for the people had noted their presence, and made a beeline straight for them, shrieking and howling like some foul creature of mythology.

"Stop where you are!" Harrison bellowed into a megaphone he had also pulled from Sloan's trunk. "Return to your homes or we'll be forced to open fire."

That warning fell on deaf ears. The mad rampage continued toward them. Sloan wondered if they were even cognizant of their actions.

"No time for talk," Sloan shouted above the din. "Open fire!"

He first shot into the air, in the vain hope that this would halt the rioters in their tracks, but to no avail. The masses were nearly upon them.

"Fire!" Sloan cried, and aimed into the crowd, firing indiscriminately. Harrison and Perez did likewise. Body after bloody body fell in a heap, but the masses still pressed forward. As more perished in a barrage of gunfire, more still came, clambering over the corpses of the fallen in mindless fashion. It was like facing the Zulu Nation at the Battle of Rorke's Drift.

"Keep firing!" Harrison yelled. "Don't let up."

The three of them pumped hot lead into the crowd, taking down dozens of assailants, but more kept coming. It was almost as though the crowd was growing, not shrinking. Were people coming in from the boroughs? Sloan thought it a likely and scary scenario.

"Where are they all coming from?" Perez cried, the desperation evident in her voice.

"We have to fall back," Sloan said. "We can't keep this up."

Harrison kept firing his assault rifle. More and more succumbed, but the growing tally of dead did nothing to stop the crowd's mad march forward. Even with their powerful weapons, eventually they would run out of ammo, and all would be lost. They were vastly outnumbered and, Sloan knew, they had no hope of surviving were they to remain.

"Get in the car you two," Harrison ordered. "I'll hold them off until I can join you."

The two cops acquiesced, but as soon as Sloan was in the driver's seat, he saw in his rear-view mirror another crowd massing at their rear.

"Oh shit," he said.

Harrison was firing at will all about him, but he suddenly found his weapon had run dry. Desperate, with no time to reload, he flailed about with his rifle, smashing it against one attacker after another.

"Quickly, get in!" Perez shouted, the assailants now all about them, bashing against their vehicle.

It was too late. As Harrison reached for the car's door handle, the massive crowd overwhelmed him and, despite his heroic efforts, he quickly disappeared under a morass of manic bodies piling upon him. Perez screamed, Sloan gunned the car into life and slammed a foot on the gas. The wheels skidded and Sloan plowed through the crowd with zero remorse, smacking into people left and right.

"We can't just leave him back there," Perez pleaded.

"It's too late for him now," Sloan said, hating the words as soon as they escaped his mouth. "We need to get back to the plaza, regroup, plan our defenses."

They finally broke free from the crowd and sped forward, back toward police headquarters, burning rubber as fast as Sloan's piece of crap would allow. He finally allowed himself a sideward glance at his partner beside him. Tears were streaming down her face, but she was clearly trying to hold it all together. She was tough. Sloan admired that, but he could tell she was broken inside. He felt the same way, he was just better at hiding it.

"This is Detective Sloan," Sloan barked into his radio. "All divisions fall back to Police Plaza. I repeat, all divisions fall back to Police Plaza. We make our stand from there."

Perez sniffed, but Sloan could tell she was still trying her hardest to collect herself. "What...what are we going to do? We're under siege. The entire city, as best I can tell, is out for blood."

Sloan shook his head, but he had no idea what to do next. He was completely shell-shocked, dead inside, like a veteran returning home from war. He was running on auto-pilot, hoping his decades-long training would steer him right, and he would find a way through to devise the next course of action. But right now he was struggling to hold it all together, just as Perez was.

He took the few corners remaining toward headquarters at high-speed, almost losing control of his wheels twice. Perez gripped her door handle frantically but said nothing. The car screeched to a halt, careening wildly before finally resting partially on the many steps leading up to the plaza.

"You're mad," Perez said, as she stumbled out of the car.

"No," Sloan said, as he retrieved the last of their weaponry and ammo from the backseat, "listen. We need to barricade this place. The only hope we have is to hold out here until the National Guard arrives."

Perez didn't look like she was buying it. "You think the local unit alone can handle this?"

He shrugged. "Honestly, I don't know. Maybe they can until the state division returns, but I can't think of anything else to do. Holding out here is our only hope."

This was sounding more and more like Rorke's Drift as time went on. Perez's jaw set in grimly, a sign she knew Sloan was right.

"Everyone needs to position their vehicles around the perimeter. Especially SWAT with their RVs," Sloan said, trying his best to take command.

Perez nodded.

"Get inside," he ordered. "Send the word through, and get everyone prepared and properly armed. I'll maneuver the car further into position and stay and direct the boys when they return."

Perez nodded again and hurried inside. As soon as she disappeared from sight, Sloan activated the call signal on his Timex watch. If ever The Wraith was needed, it was now.

~ Chapter 5 ~

The Fisky Building was an elegant sandstone structure in the heart of the city's financial district. It was home to many of the city's movers and shakers, including stockbrokers, prestigious law firms, and high-priced accountants. Its edifice was adorned with mighty pillars of Spanish marble, which gave the building an air of a flamboyant European palace.

The Wraith and Lady Wraith stood atop the adjoining, much taller Wilson Tower; a more modern, expressionistic-styled office complex, which looked rather odd alongside its more aged neighbor. The Wraith was perched on the edge, his foot up against the railing and his cape billowing around him. He stared down at the Fisky rooftop.

"The Fisky Building is fully tenanted," Lady Wraith said, joining her partner. "The basement has nothing but parking spaces. There's no way the Cobra could be hiding here."

The Wraith remained silent, focusing intensely on the rooftop opposite. Something wasn't right and felt unnatural. He'd sensed it the moment they had arrived. He flicked his night-vision lenses on. Still nothing.

"Darling, did you hear me?" Lady Wraith said.

What was he feeling? He couldn't understand it. But there was something there, right in front of his eyes. He just couldn't make it out.

"Darling?"

Just then, a faint drizzle started to fall. The Wraith barely noticed it at first. Then, the drizzle began to increase.

There, he thought.

It was faint, the barest impression of water trickling on and around a hitherto invisible shape, but as soon as The Wraith became aware of it, the structure appeared to him as though by magic. It was a large pagoda-style building of wood and plaster, built atop the Fisky Building without anyone even being aware of its existence. The Cobra, with his powerful mental abilities, had shielded it from all of the world. The Wraith's eyes bulged open at the realization of it all.

"Darling, you're scaring me," Lady Wraith said at last.

"Don't you see it?" The Wraith said, turning to face his partner.

"See what? The Fisky rooftop?"

"You don't see it?" The Wraith said, incredulous, but realizing he alone had broken through the Cobra's mental facade. "Nobody sees it, but I see it."

Without another thought, he leaped from his vantage point, out into the night sky, landing with a forward roll onto the sodden asphalt of the Fisky roof. He quickly stood and marched toward the door several feet in front of him. He heard Lady Wraith land behind him and made his way inside the pagoda.

Once inside, he strode down a lengthy corridor festooned with lit torches and oriental flourishes. He noted a musty odor permeating the structure, then detected Lady Wraith's presence at his rear. His Héron Marinor watch then indicated a message. He promptly glanced at the dial. It was from Sloan. He would have to wait.

"I can't believe it," Lady Wraith said under her breath. "To think this was here, completely invisible to all."

"Be on your guard," The Wraith warned. "The Cobra may sense our arrival."

Nevertheless, they marched forth, down the hallway, which twisted and turned before arriving at an open-plan room with a raised platform at the far end where an ornate throne sat regally. The ceiling was curved in concave fashion with hardwood slats, but there was no sign of the Cobra. Two open doors were positioned on either side of the platform.

"You were expected," a rough voice emanated throughout the room.

In turn, a series of burly men—all outfitted identically to Blackstorm—appeared from both of the open doorways, marching in unison one-by-one. They kept on coming, an army of Blackstorms, until finally they stood in perfect formation before the platform, facing the two heroes.

"The master fears no one," one Blackstorm said, as he stepped forth from the dozen or so congregated there. "But he does respect you and your ability to be a thorn in his side."

"Where is the Cobra?" The Wraith said, ignoring the lackey's speech.

"You will be a thorn no longer," the Blackstorm leader said. "It ends here, now!"

The Blackstorms emitted some form of call to arms and prepared themselves for battle. The Wraith glanced at Lady Wraith, who flexed her muscles. They knew they were in for the fight of their lives.

* * * * * *

"The situation is becoming serious, sir."

Robert Latham turned from the window behind his desk and faced his latest assistant, John Carruthers, now outfitted in a superbly tailored suit mirroring his own. "Is Smithers ready with the chopper?" 10

"He's approaching the building now, sir," Carruthers said.

Latham smiled wanly, rounded his desk, and approached his assistant. "There's no hope we can hold out here?"

"The building is locked down, sir, roller shutters in place at every ground floor door and window."

"Then why the sudden need for evacuation?" Latham said.

"We don't know if the barricades will hold," Carruthers said. "They weren't constructed to withstand a mass insurrection. And then there's the matter of onsite staff."

"What do you mean?"

"Whatever is afflicting the people outside could start affecting the staff. Or even us. I cannot guarantee your continued safety here."

Latham nodded sternly. He understood, and acknowledged the opinion of the man who had once been one of his armed, and well trained, guards. He had also recently saved his life.

"Smithers has arrived, sir," Carruthers said a few moments later, tapping at a radio earpiece.

"Good. We'll be safe at the bunker at my home. We'll ride out this nightmare there."

He allowed Carruthers to lead him from his office and along the hallway out toward the elevator. Soon, they would be safely in the air and heading towards his newly rebuilt home. His compound. He wondered how long they would have to hunker down there. It was well equipped for such emergencies. That didn't concern him. But whatever was afflicting Metro City–*his* city–was unfathomable.

He could only hope it would soon be over.

* * * * * *

A storm was brewing. What started as a slight drizzle had morphed into a steady rain, then a torrential downpour. Now, thunder roiled through the night sky, and streaks of lightning sent almighty bolts of electricity in every direction.

The inclement weather failed to deter a semi-trailer parking by the disused Christopher Docks. A series, perhaps a dozen or so, of black-clad men–almost ninja-like–emerged from the trailer and made their way steadily down to Wharf Five where a small, rusty boat lay docked, thrashing violently against the rotting, wooden wharf. Bringing up the rear was a Blackstorm, following his men toward the boat. 11

"Quickly," he ordered, "we must retrieve our precious cargo and begone from here. The city is waylaid, yes, but The Wraith and his team can never be underestimated."

A half-dozen ninjas descended onto the craft and disappeared below deck. The rest remained on deck, with one stationed on either side of Blackstorm on the wharf. Within moments, the men emerged carrying a large wooden crate.

"Be careful," Blackstorm said, thunder failing to dent the power of his speech. "Our lives depend on the safe passage of this cargo."

All the ninjas then took hold of the crate and carefully maneuvered it up to the wharf for Blackstorm's close inspection.

"It is undamaged," he said with satisfaction. "The cargo is within?"

"Yes, Blackstorm. I have seen to it personally," one ninja spoke in a clipped tone.

"Good," Blackstorm said. "Place it onboard the truck. Take all the necessary precautions. Our master's destiny awaits us."

The men did as they were bidden. The storm continued to thrash forcefully through the inky sky, perhaps a sign of the carnage that was to come.

* * * * * *

"Is everything in readiness?" the Cobra said, with just a hint of impatience.

"Yes, master," Max replied, standing over a large, metallic sphere that was almost Meccano-like in construction. "The sphere is complete."

The Cobra allowed himself a brief smile. Everything was proceeding as planned. "You have done well. Remain here until the cargo arrives shortly. Then you may install it, in preparation for the next phase of the operation."

"Yes, master," Max said in sotto voice.

The Cobra turned away from Max and again allowed himself some sense of gratification. His destiny was right there in front of him. He could almost taste the blood of his victims, falling one-by-one, at his feet. Domination would soon be his and he would finally take his rightful place as ruler of all life. He shuddered with anticipation.

Nothing would stop him now. Not even The Wraith. His destiny would not allow it.

~ Chapter 6 ~

Tensions were at breaking point, but neither party had stirred more than an inch. The Wraith wondered who would move first. Muscles were tensed, positions shuffled. Suddenly, the stalemate was broken with a sharp cry from the lead Blackstorm, and the rest then charged at the heroes, ready to tear them apart.

They came at them in full force, attacking left and right. The Wraith and Lady Wraith lashed out with fists and feet, battling as never before. He knew the time for mercy was over. There was too much at stake. It was life or death, and the Blackstorms would take no prisoners.

Each Blackstorm was as skilled and powerful as the previous ones they had encountered. Blows were parried and evaded as best they could, but others connected. Their armored uniforms offered some protection, but The Wraith was unable to prevent several strikes to his face. Blood trickled from his nose.

He realized the only form of defense was offence, and decided to attack at all costs. His punches struck with such power that the knuckles of his hand cracked each time. Teeth were fragmented, jaws were shattered. He continued, not daring to pause for breath. Another Blackstorm and another. A kick to the knee, smashing it, felled one, a punch to the solar plexus another. The Wraith held nothing back. It was bone-crunching brutality.

Lady Wraith cried out, causing The Wraith to glance over at her. It was his undoing, as two Blackstorms used the momentary loss of concentration to lash out in unison, flooring him with a series of expert strikes. The Wraith fell to his knees, blood oozing from his mouth. He spotted Lady Wraith, likewise, struggling to stand on an injured right leg. Boots lashed out, catching him in the back and torso. He felt a rib snap. He coughed up more blood.

We have to go on, The Wraith thought. *We can't let it all end here or the Cobra will slaughter millions.*

"Lady Wraith," The Wraith called out in anguish. "Fry!" The thought of such a final solution sickened him, but they had little choice now.

She managed to regain her footing and activated the Eyes of Judgment on her chest. Hers were an invention of Max's, with which she could either temporarily blind an opponent with its intense flash of LED light, or obliterate them using a unique combination of strobing light and their patented flash powder. The latter was always a last resort option, but this was a last resort situation.

She screamed in fury as she bathed attacker after attacker with her deathly Judgment Stare. Each shuddered briefly before incinerating on the spot. Lady Wraith kept up her assault, with more Blackstorms engaging in attack, but all were dealt with in the same fatal fashion.

The Wraith dragged himself back into the fray, forcing himself into action once more, against the pain, smiting opponents left and right with vicious blows.

"We cannot fail the master," the Blackstorm leader cried out. "We must defeat the infidels."

Despite her injuries, Lady Wraith pressed forward and continued her deadly assault, felling every assailant. The Wraith fought on with savage strength, fueled by anger and adrenalin.

Ultimately, after all the mayhem, after all about them had fallen, one Blackstorm remained standing. His armor was damaged, and he was panting heavily, but he stood proud and appeared ready to fight to the death. The Wraith wiped the blood away from his lips. The taste of it stung his throat. Lady Wraith limped into position alongside him. They were injured and weary, but one adversary remained.

"Your brethren are vanquished," The Wraith boomed, bringing the Eyes of Judgment to fiery life. "You are abandoned and alone. You will now face judgment, and you will tell me what I wish to know!"

The remaining Blackstorm merely grunted and returned to a battle stance. He wasn't going down without a fight. The Wraith growled and acquiesced. He launched into the fray with a renewed vigor, not allowing the Blackstorm even a moment to collect himself, landing a side kick to the stomach, and a powerful right and left to the jaw. The Blackstorm attempted a punch of his own, but The Wraith caught the arm and plunged an elbow down onto it, snapping it in two.

The Blackstorm cried out in pain and staggered back. The villain looked left and right, as though expecting assistance from either doorway. None came. With Lady Wraith watching on, The Wraith continued the onslaught, raining mighty blow after blow upon the hapless and obviously tired villain. At last, the Blackstorm dropped to his knees. With a growl, The Wraith ripped the villain's mask from him, revealing yet another non-descript young man of Asiatic appearance.

"You will tell me what I want to know," The Wraith moaned, latching on to the Blackstorm's head and forcing it toward the Eyes of Judgment. "Where is Max Horton?"

The Blackstorm thrashed about, as though trying to break free from The Wraith's thrall, but it proved impossible. Once in The Wraith's grasp, in his Judgment Stare, there was no escape. Finally, the Blackstorm's movement began to cease.

"I...I..." the Blackstorm muttered.

"Tell me!" The Wraith repeated.

"I...I...cannot..." the Blackstorm said, as though he were fighting some raging, internal war.

Then he began to gurgle. His body went rigid and, before The Wraith could say another word, he collapsed to the floor, spasming in savage seizures. Then, his body went limp, and all was silent. Lady Wraith rushed over, as The Wraith deactivated the Eyes.

"He's dead," Lady Wraith said, feeling for a pulse. "Some sort of fit, perhaps. Not poison for once."

"Or the Cobra exerting his ultimate control," The Wraith said. "Either way, we've learned nothing here."

Lady Wraith stood precariously, favoring one leg.

"You're hurt," The Wraith said.

"No more than you, I'm sure," she said. "I'll heal. But what's our next step?"

The Wraith remained silent for a moment, looked about, and examined the room more closely. Then he pointed to one of the open doors. "We search this location thoroughly. There must be some evidence here."

He raced for the door and plunged through it, Lady Wraith hobbling as best she could behind him. Another hallway greeted them, curving ahead of them to the left. The Wraith wondered if it was a circular path leading back around to the room where they had just come. No matter, he followed the path. Up ahead was a stairway leading above. The remainder of the hallway did indeed lead, he could tell, back to the scene of their brutal combat.

"We go up," he said.

It was a steep but short flight of stairs. They arrived at an upper level more ornately decorated than below, the far wall adorned with a larger, much more elaborate throne bejeweled in precious stones. Lady Wraith gasped, for there, seated on the throne, was the Cobra himself, with Max standing stoically by his side. The villain appeared as formidable, as arrogant, as always; however, The Wraith noted that there were now substantial streaks of gray flecked throughout his temples. They were not as large at their recent encounter. The Wraith couldn't help but wonder if the Cobra's mental control over the entire city was somehow draining his strength. A potential advantage like that could prove valuable.

"I continue to underestimate your reserves of strength," the Cobra said heartily. "You have proven superior to my trusted warriors again."

"This is between us," The Wraith said, "as it always has been. Release Max and let us settle this."

"This infidel?" the Cobra said, motioning to Max. "He means nothing to me. Merely a means to an end. And that end is now complete."

The Cobra's right eye gleamed in the light and Max reached up to his throat, as though he was now choking.

"Max!" The Wraith screamed.

The Cobra raised his right hand, and The Wraith found himself frozen in place, unable to move. He felt sure Lady Wraith was similarly afflicted. Once again, his archenemy had bested him. He grew tired of feeling so helpless, of *being* so helpless. He was sure this would now be the end.

"You have been an entertaining diversion, I must confess," the Cobra said, as he approached the two of them. "But destiny awaits only one man. Soon, this city will be annihilated, and all in this country will then bow down before me, before my might, lest they suffer the same fate as Metro City."

The Wraith struggled within himself, but the Cobra's will was too strong. He was utterly within his enemy's power. And Max still suffered in the background.

"And the world itself will then follow suit. All will realize their only hope for survival is to kneel before Abdelkrim, their one true savior."

Darkness beckoned. All hope was lost. Then a thought popped into his mind. Could he, perhaps, activate the Eyes of Judgment? Was that, too, restricted by the Cobra's subjugation? He had to try. The Eyes of Judgment burst into ardent life, the Cobra caught completely unawares. The villain staggered back from the burst. Just a little, but enough for The Wraith to break free from his mental hold.

"Abdelkrim! Let us finish this now!"

"I would grind your bones into the dust," the Cobra snarled. "But not yet. My destiny is not yet fulfilled. Your time is still to come." He again raised a hand, and darkness embraced The Wraith like the most passionate of lovers.

The Wraith's eyes burst open. He waved his arms about. He was free. There was no sign of his adversary, and no indication of how long he had been out. At a guess, it wasn't long, but he couldn't be sure of that. Lady Wraith murmured something. He didn't waste a moment, and rushed over to check on his fallen friend. Max was unconscious, but alive. A pulse, although weakened, was still evident. However, his breathing was erratic. The Wraith didn't hesitate and started administering mouth-to-mouth to revive his friend.

After some moments, Max began coughing and sputtering. He sat upright, but it was instantly evident he was still under the Cobra's control. He was pale, which was not surprising under the circumstances, but his features were deadpan. His eyes showed no sign of active consciousness, almost as though his soul was being drained before their very eyes. Max's eyes then began to droop, and he slowly tilted sideways.

"Max!" The Wraith shouted. "MAX!"

He gripped his friend by the shoulders.

"What's happening?" Lady Wraith said.

"It's as though his life force is draining away," The Wraith explained.

He glanced at Lady Wraith, and noted her frantic expression. He knew how she felt. Their friend was dying, and there was nothing they could do about it.

Or was there?

The Eyes of Judgment sparked into life once again.

"What are you doing?" Lady Wraith said, her voice tinged with desperation.

"Playing a hunch," The Wraith said. "I saved Max's life once before, many years ago in London. I'm hoping–"

"For the same result," Lady Wraith finished his sentence.

The Wraith clutched Max's head and brought it down to face the full strength of his Judgment Stare. The Irishman was still conscious, but barely.

"My friend, your soul will be cleansed once again. No more will you be under the control of one who is evil. You will be free!" The Wraith said.

Max squirmed and roiled in The Wraith's embrace, as the mystical energies from the Eyes of Judgment flowed around and within him all at once. The Irishman's eyes bulged wide and his face contorted in abject horror. He screamed in agony.

"Chief," Max finally said, sweat pouring from his brow. "You've done it, I'm free, I'm-"

His voice trailed away as he fell to the floor, comatose.

"Max!" The Wraith said. He crouched down and checked on his friend. His vitals were strong, his breathing sound, but he was unconscious.

"Call Dr. Needham, tell him to rush to our home and bring whatever he needs with him, no matter the cost. With the current situation in the city, I think it best we care for Max there." 12

Lady Wraith nodded. "What about Simpson?"

"Check on his condition. If it's safe to move him, arrange it with Needham." The Wraith started for the exit.

"Wait!" Lady Wraith cried. "Where are you going?"

"Sloan called. I'm needed at police headquarters."

~ Chapter 7 ~

"**B**arricades are in place, sir. We even found some sandbags to put into position."

Sloan acknowledged the young constable with a slight nod. He estimated him to be no more than twenty-two-years-old. "Every vehicle we have?"

"Yes, sir," the constable said.

"Good," Sloan said, feeling a mixture of satisfaction and trepidation. He knew what was coming and it turned his stomach.

Every available officer, uniformed and plain clothed, congregated in the Metro Police Plaza foyer. All were heavily armed. Several were wounded. Sloan had taken unofficial command.

"Everybody upstairs to the second floor," Sloan yelled. "Man every window facing the street. If we're lucky, the barricades–and our firepower–will hold them off."

"But, sir," another, slightly older, constable said, getting into Sloan's face a little, "we can't do that. These are innocent people; we'd be murdering innocent civilians."

"Constable," Sloan said, gripping the officer's shoulders. "I know how you feel. They *are* innocent people, caught up in this horrific nightmare. But the reality is they're out to kill. Whatever's afflicting them, they will massacre us if we don't fight back." Sloan turned to face the others. "We have zero time to think of another solution. Right now, there *is* no other solution. We fight back with lethal force. There is no other way."

The constable appeared solemn, dropped his shoulders, and nodded meekly in agreement. Sloan slapped him on the back in a further attempt to reassure him.

"Okay, upstairs, into position. We won't have long to wait, I'm sure."

Everyone marched up the stairs at speed, like an army platoon preparing for battle. Sloan brought up the rear. He wondered if this was how commanding officers felt directing the troops on the front line. It was a weird analogy for modern-day America, but no less valid.

He made sure everyone was in position and no window was left unmanned or vantage point unfilled. He even had snipers positioned at various points on the rooftop, lest by some chance the zombies–for what else could they be called–somehow breached their defenses and made their way round the back of the complex.

"I see some movement up ahead," a voice rang out over Sloan's radio.

"Stay sharp, and keep your eyes peeled. All right, team," he said, shuffling back and forth behind everyone. "This is our moment. If we fail here, all is lost. Not just our lives, but potentially everyone in this city. Our loved ones. We make our stand here and we prevail...because we have to."

"Yes, sir," came the unified reply.

Perez sidled alongside her partner. "I can't believe what we're facing here. It's like a war zone. We're at war with...the people of this city?"

"None of this makes any sense," Sloan said. "Something has been done to these poor people. Someone has done this. I want answers, but...we don't have time right now to look for them."

"Large crowd massing on the northern end of the street," a voice came through on Sloan's radio. "They're heading this way."

"This is it," he told Perez. "Be prepared for anything."

Sloan's muscles went rigid. Sweat beaded his brow. He turned left and right, inspecting his troops. Everyone was on high alert. It was now or never.

"They're almost upon us," the voice came through the radio again. "Heading right for us."

A shot rang out, then another and another. The snipers on the roof, Sloan realized. The detective gripped his weapon, peered out a window alongside a uniformed officer. The crowd approached the barricades and, upon reaching it, attempted to climb over the various vehicles congregated there.

"Open fire!" Sloan cried.

Every officer, man and woman, let fly with a barrage of weaponry. The sound of so much gunfire in such proximity was deafening, but on and on they continued. Body after body fell in turn.

"It's like shooting ducks in a barrel," one officer shouted, perhaps a little too gleefully.

"Keep firing, don't let up. We cannot let them breach our defenses," Sloan shouted, vowing to have a word with that officer if and when they survived this.

It was a slaughter of epic proportions. The fallen numbered in the dozens, but still they came, wildly, madly.

"There are more marching from both directions," came the voice again through Sloan's radio. "Just plowing toward us."

Sloan turned to Perez. "It's like the entire city is heading here. Even from the outer boroughs."

"We're going to run out of ammo," Perez said, her features etched with great concern.

"Where's the bloody local NG unit?" Sloan barked to nobody in particular. There was nobody amongst them with any immediate answers.

"They're still coming," a plain clothed detective announced from further into the room.

"Keep firing," Sloan repeated. What else could he say? Their only hope was the crowd would begin to thin out before their ammunition failed, or they decided to retreat. These were forlorn hopes, perhaps, but it was all they had. So Sloan adhered to his own mantra.

He kept firing.

* * * * * *

The snipers on the police headquarters rooftop facing the building fired repeatedly at the billowing swarm of bodies, their pinpoint aim causing numerous fatalities. And yet, onward they progressed, wanton death and destruction seemingly their only aim, their own pointless deaths of no apparent concern to them.

A dark cloaked shape suddenly dropped down amongst the sharpshooters out of nowhere.

"Geez!" one sniper yelped.

It was The Wraith. He peered over the building's edge and took stock of the situation. It was bad. There were hundreds of people massing below in the street, all eager to invade the Plaza and cause unmitigated harm to its inhabitants. It was the January 6 insurrection on steroids. But there was some hope.

"I've reconnoitered the area," The Wraith said to all around him. "The crowds are thinning in both directions leading from downtown. If we can hold the line for another...half hour or so–"

"We may not have the ammo to last that long," the sniper nearest The Wraith said.

"Then it's my job to give you that time."

He pulled his grapnel gun from his belt, attached one end of the line to the edge of the building, and, holding the other end, launched himself into the open air. The line grew taut and the gun, attached to his belt, slowed his descent.

With bullets flying all around, he landed right in the heart of the zombie army, quickly lashing out with a series of intricate martial arts maneuvers to allow himself some breathing space. He knew what he had to do. He only hoped he had enough flash powder on hand to buy them all the time they needed.

A series of zombies–their expressions wild and aggressive–fixed their attention on The Wraith and diverted them from attacking the police. Thankfully, the police had stopped firing in his direction, allowing him to work more freely. He pulled a handful of small capsules from his belt and lobbed them at the feet of his oncoming attackers. A fiery burst erupted from the ground, enveloping a series of zombies in its turbulent energies, utterly consuming them, reducing them to little more than ash.

The Wraith repeated this move, tossing capsule after capsule at the feet of all those around him. One by one, they fell victim to the Dread Avenger's wrath. Every time they swarmed, they were dealt with accordingly. He was grateful the attackers were so close together that the capsules took out several at a time. It made an impossible task slightly more doable.

* * * * * *

"Do not fire on The Wraith!" Sloan said.

He and his team watched on with awe and apprehension as the Dread Avenger administered lethal justice to all and sundry. It was an astonishing display of power and ruthlessness that caused even Sloan to shudder briefly.

"He's just one man," Perez said after a few moments of witnessing the carnage, skepticism tinging her voice. "What can he hope to accomplish?"

"He isn't just one man," Sloan replied. "He's The Wraith."

* * * * * *

Still they came, rushing at The Wraith from left and right, death writ on their faces. More flash pellets were thrown at them, and all were destroyed.

The Wraith retrieved the last series of pellets he had on hand. There were still too many zombies to deal with. Swiftly, he returned the pellets to their pouch, and launched himself into physical attack. The only advantage his enemies had was force of number. Individually, they were an unskilled rabble, no real threat to The Wraith at all. But he was injured–a broken rib, lacerations to his face and body–and bone tired.

He pushed the pain and weariness into a corner of his mind and locked it away, a technique he had conquered long ago, and dealt with each zombie with bone-crushing efficiency. As shots again rang out, dealing with the mindless on the fringes of the battle, The Wraith let loose with violence unprecedented in his nature. Necks were snapped, limbs were broken, blood was spilled. When any other man would have fallen from sheer exhaustion alone, The Wraith pushed on, his vast willpower pressing him onward.

It was then he pulled out the last remaining flash pellets from his belt and tossed them with pinpoint accuracy at those left standing. They suffered the same fate as all those before.

Enraged, adrenalin alone fueling him to go on, he swiveled about, his arms raised, ready to continue fighting...but there was nobody left. It took him a few moments to realize, but ultimately, he finally lowered his arms, his body trembling and his muscles aching. He had given all, and then some, and had nothing left in the tank. Exhaustion gripped him, and darkness began to overpower him.

He started to inch away, thoughts of escaping home or anywhere else overwhelming him, but his body wasn't cooperating.

The last thing he remembered was a weak sun slowly arching to his right.

~ Chapter 8 ~

It was bitterly cold. A blustery wind cut through him like a knife. A thick fog wafted about the plateau. Snow began to fall. Despite the inclement weather, Paul was out chopping wood as he always did every morning. He enjoyed the work and the bracing conditions as he flexed his muscles, allowing his mind to relax and wander. Paul often thought of his childhood, and the loneliness and confusion he'd experienced living with parents that never had time for him. In his early adulthood, he had also felt a yawning chasm in his heart and soul, and an inability to fill that void with anything of substance. How odd, he thought, that he finally felt an inner peace here, on the peak of Emba Soira in Eritrea. His long quest for enlightenment had brought him to this place. 13

"How curious to find you here," a booming voice echoed around him.

Paul dropped his axe, looking around for the source of this intrusion, but saw nothing. He rubbed his eyes. Was the thin air up here playing tricks on him?

"Especially as it was not *you* that visited this place," the voice said.

Paul took a backward step for there before him the fog was morphing into a shape. It was a face. The Cobra.

"You are not the Paul Sanderson that I confronted in the desert, nor the one who faced me here at the old man's temple," the Cobra said. "These memories are not truly yours. You are a pretender, living a false life."

Paul realized this was a memory, a dream, a product of his mind. And he knew this man. Abdelkrim. The enforcer of Eritrea, the terrorist from Iran. And he knew him as The Wraith's arch-nemesis, the Cobra.

"Your words are meaningless to me," Paul said. "I know who I am. I have come to terms with my identity and my life's work."

The Cobra snorted. "You are nothing. You are an infidel who received the gift that was rightfully mine. The old man was a fool."

"You are not worthy of it," Paul said. "You would despoil everything the old man held dear."

"It is of no matter," the Cobra said. "The power I received has given me a mastery of all life. The descendant of Tamerlane deserves nothing less."

"Why are you here, Abdelkrim? Your attempts at tormenting me have failed."

The Cobra's image smiled lasciviously, a somewhat disturbing sight. "Even in your dreams, you cannot escape me. I can invade these as I do your waking mind. You are nothing to me. No distance can force me from controlling you if I so wish it. You are a mere puppet, whom I choose to play with at my whim."

"You don't frighten me," Paul said.

"Your false bravado is predictable," the Cobra mocked, "but of no concern to me. I will leave you with this parting missive."

Paul's eyes narrowed.

"I am coming for you..."

The Cobra's voice trailed off into the wind, and his face disappeared into the fog.

"Yah!"

Paul sat bolt upright, sweat pouring from his face. He breathed heavily, and he was drenched from head to toe.

"It's all right, darling. You're safe at home."

Leena sat down next to him and he realized where he was. He was at home, in his own bed, and beautiful sunshine was streaming through the expansive window opposite. His torso was tightly strapped.

"How...why...?"

Leena gently stroked his cheek. "Sloan brought you home. In all the confusion, nobody noticed. You collapsed in the street after all that you did. You saved them all."

It was then that he remembered the awful reality of what had happened. He had murdered–yes, murdered–hundreds of people. The thought of it hurt him more than any physical injury could. Leena must have seen his despondency.

"You did what you had to do to save many," Leena tried to console him. It wasn't working. "You did more than any man could be expected to do."

"All those people, Leena, are dead." It was as though a part of him had died as well. Then he snapped himself back to the issue at hand. "Max? Simpson?"

"Both are well and here in the house," Leena said. "Dr. Needham has taken expert care of them. He administered to your wounds as well."

"What time is it?"

"It's still morning. Emily was still asleep last I checked."

That was a name he had not heard in a long time, or so it seemed. In this time of tragedy, he needed his family. And the Cobra was still at large. He jumped from his bed and headed for the ensuite bathroom.

"Hey!" Leena complained. "You still need some rest."

Paul ignored her and went to shower and shave with his Rockwell T2 razor. He noticed the bruising to his face and a gash to his cheek. How would he explain this? Raising an eyebrow, he exited, dressed in a navy polo shirt and khaki chinos, and went to his daughter's bedroom. He knocked and entered with a smile. Emily sat up in her bed and stretched.

"Good morning, sleepyhead," Paul said.

"I always sleep so well here," she said, returning his smile with a bigger one of her own. She then noticed his injuries. "You're hurt." Her smile vanished.

"I'm okay. I slipped on the staircase." It was the best he could do on the spur of the moment.

"Oh no," she said with some concern. "You should be more careful. Stairs can be slippery."

He smiled again. "I know that...now. I'll be more careful in the future." He stroked her cheek. "Time for breakfast, I think."

"Are you cooking again?"

"You bet."

"Oh goodie," Emily said, bounding from her bed and into her slippers. "Let's go." They descended the staircase extra cautiously. "Will your...butt-ler...be feeling better soon?"

"Oh yes, he'll be fine," Paul said with a slight chuckle. "He's home now and resting comfortably." He enjoyed holding his daughter's hand.

"But you'll be cooking pancakes for me, right?"

"For as long as you want."

* * * * * *

When their meal was over, Leena appeared in the breakfast room.

"Anything for you, darling?" Paul said.

"Just some coffee," Leena replied. "I'll help myself."

"Emily Roseanne–" Paul started.

"You can call me Emily," she said. "My mommy used to call me Emily Roseanne when she was angry with me."

Paul laughed. "Okay, Emily. She wasn't angry with you very often, was she?"

"Of course not. I'm a good girl," she said.

Paul laughed again. "Of course. Now, could you please keep Leena company here? I have to go check in on Simpson upstairs."

"Sure. Can I have another hot chocolate, please?" Emily said eagerly.

"You certainly may," Leena said, heading into the kitchen to make it and her coffee. She gave Paul a reassuring look. He knew it was fine to check on his friend.

He headed upstairs and traversed the hallways to arrive at Simpson's quarters. He opened the door an inch. Dr. Needham was there checking on his patient. From the look of him, he'd been there at his post half the night.

"Doctor," Paul said. "Is it all right to come in?"

"Of course. He's sleeping still."

Paul moved slowly inside and looked at his longtime employee and friend sorrowfully. He was sleeping in a hospital bed hooked up to a variety of machines. "How is he?"

"Broken neck, as initially suspected," Dr. Needham explained. "But no major damage to the spinal column, thank goodness. There's bruising, and it's heavily inflamed, but that will settle in time. All he needs is rest to heal his wounds."

"He'll get all the rest he needs. Is it safe to keep him here?" Paul said.

"Oh yes, he's out of any danger, I think. These monitors here are just in case he had worsened on the journey over here. I see no evidence of that thus far."

Paul took a deep breath of relief.

"Your friend, though, Max Horton," Dr. Needham said.

"Yes?"

"Well...I don't really know what's wrong with him. He appears to be in some sort of coma, but medically speaking, I can find nothing wrong with him. It's a mystery to me," the doctor said, scratching his head. "He's in his room, resting as well."

"Thank you, doctor," Paul said. "Thank you for patching me up as well."

"It's not the first time," Dr. Needham said with a wry grin. "And I'm sure it won't be the last."

Paul smiled in acknowledgement.

"I'll be heading home now. I'd like to catch up on some lost sleep. I'll be back later today to check on both my patients. Don't hesitate to call at any time if needed."

"Will do," Paul said, "and thank you again."

Dr. Needham grabbed his coat and quickly exited.

Paul turned his attention back to Simpson, his neck wrapped carefully in a padded brace. Paul sat in the chair alongside Simpson's bed and took his butler's hand in his. He noted how coarse and wrinkled the fingers were. Simpson had been a war veteran and the family butler for decades. His hands were evidence of all his hard work.

Memories flooded his mind of Paul Sanderson's–the original's–life with Simpson. His eyes filled with tears. Upon the death of his parents, Simpson had become his de facto mother and father all in one. He'd received more love from this old man in one day than he had ever received from his parents.

"Remember that time when you found me playing in the garden with a tablecloth wrapped around my neck?" Paul laughed at the memory. "Did you ever imagine we'd be here like this right now? That my life would eventually mirror that day's play?" He gently squeezed Simpson's hand. "I know I'm not...really *that* Paul that you loved and nurtured all those years ago, but...I have all his memories. I have his emotions and a part of his soul. He lives on in me, and...well...what I'm trying to say is...I love you, Simpson. I can't imagine life without you. You've always been there for me. Taken care of me, then and now. You need to get well. This family needs you, now more than ever."

At that moment, Simpson tightened his grip slightly on Paul's hand. Paul's heart leaped with joy.

"I will...always be there for you...son," Simpson croaked, though his eyes remained shut. He had heard every word Paul had said.

Tears of joy flooded Paul's face. He wiped them away as he stood. "You continue to rest well, Simpson. It's our turn to take care of you now." He gently rested his hand briefly on Simpson's shoulder, then turned and left.

Quickly, his thoughts turned to Max, and the nightmare the city, the nation, and the world still faced. He made his way over to his friend's room, and found him in much the same condition, appearance wise at least, as Simpson. He was lying in his bed, attached to some machines, seemingly sleeping comfortably. Paul sat down beside his friend. If there were any answers to the crisis now engulfing them all, they resided in Max's mind. He needed his friend now like never before.

"No, leave me alone!" Max shouted, his eyes still shut tight.

"Max," Paul said with some alarm. "Max, wake up. Come back to us."

The Irishman sat bolt upright, his eyes still closed. He screamed. Then opened his eyes.

"Max," Paul said again. "Are you...are you all right?"

"Chief?" Max said a little weakly. "Is that you?"

"Yes, Max, I'm here. You're home safe and sound."

Max's face clouded over with a mixture of fear and horror. It was scary to see.

"I...I couldn't stop him," the Irishman said in a tone of remorse. "He overpowered me, right here in this house, so long ago. He took control of me. I relayed information to him..." He began to sob.

"It's all right. You had no way of fighting the Cobra. He's too powerful. You mustn't blame yourself."

Max buried his head in his hands, sobbing. "No, no, you don't understand. It isn't just that."

"What are you talking about?" Paul said.

"I've created an atomic bomb for him!"

~ Chapter 9 ~

Those words shook Paul to his very core. The implications were truly horrendous.

"What? How?" was all he could utter.

"The Cobra arranged delivery of some weapons-grade plutonium," Max recounted. "I had already built him a Berilium Sphere to house it, and had just completed installation of the radioactive material when you rescued me."

Paul felt sure his mouth had dropped open. The Cobra, in possession of a working atomic bomb? This nightmare was never ending. What in Heaven's name could they do? His mind reeled; all hope had dissipated. They had lost, utterly and irrevocably. But then he caught himself. No, he mustn't believe that.

"Max, the Cobra thinks you're dead. Surely we can use that to our advantage," he said.

Max's face brightened. "Of course. I know what he's planning, where the bomb will be located, and when."

"Excellent. Let's get to work."

* * * * * *

There had been no further attacks on police headquarters. This–lull?–in activity had allowed Sloan to direct something of a clean-up of the street facing the police building. Hundreds, if not thousands, of bodies had to be removed. It was unbearable to watch, but it was a job that had to be done. When the National Guard unit finally arrived, they were assigned the dreadful task. Under the circumstances, Sloan decided it was the least they could do.

Once the last body had been escorted away, Sloan turned to Perez and wiped the sweat from his brow. He was done in. He needed a drink, preferably a beer. And he wanted to sleep for twenty hours straight, if not longer.

"I don't want to go through something like that again," Perez said, her face mirroring Sloan's emotions. What they had been forced to do was unspeakable. All the arguments in favor of their course of action resonated in his brain. He recognized their truth, but it didn't make him feel any better. He wondered if anything ever could.

"I can't fathom any of this," Sloan finally said. "What the hell did we just do? What was it all about?"

"Survival, Bob. Pure and simple. Us or them."

"Yeah," Sloan said, again seeing the truth of her words, but still feeling awful. "I just hate myself right now."

"What about these barricades?" Perez said, pointing to all the hemmed in vehicles surrounding Metro Police Plaza. All were damaged in some way. "Dare we move them?"

"Not yet," Sloan said. "We can't be sure there won't be another attack." He spoke to the other officers around them. "Check those cars over there, see that everything is still as locked in place as possible, then get back inside. I have a feeling this isn't over."

The others nodded and, despite their intense weariness, proceeded to do their jobs. Sloan took one last look at the sun, now around a quarter of the way up in the sky. The warmth on his face felt good, but it wasn't enough to scorch the sense of guilt he felt from his soul.

It was a feeling he knew would live with him forever.

* * * * * *

Max and Paul were ensconced in the Lair, trying furiously to ascertain their next course of action. They faced two problems, and both were major crises in their own right. They had to find some way of breaking the Cobra's control over the city's population. And, of course, they had to find the atomic bomb and defuse it before it was too late.

"Well, I think I have one thing sorted out," Max said after some deliberation. "If we can patch into the city's typhoon early warning system..."

"The loud speakers scattered throughout the city?"

"...and flood the city with an intense white noise..."

"White noise?" Paul interrupted again.

"...I think that would act as a deterrent to the Cobra's mental control."

None of that made sense to Paul, but he always trusted his friend's genius.

"I don't have time to explain it now," Max said, perhaps noticing a look of confusion on Paul's face. "It's to do with the equilibrium of the inner ear."

"That's okay, I trust you, Max," Paul said. "How quickly can we get that done?"

"Not long. I just have to tinker with the exact frequency and volume. And then just play it on a loop for as long as possible."

"Good," Paul said, feeling like they were finally getting somewhere, and finally gaining the upper hand. "But then we have an even bigger problem."

"We have a little time," Max said. "The Cobra isn't planning to plant the bomb until late tonight, and he has an escape route ready."

Paul shook his head. The horror of it all was palpable. He looked down at his Erebus Ascent watch. It was close to 4:00PM. They had only hours to achieve their goals.

"Get to work on the white noise; we don't have a moment to lose. And then where do we go?"

"Latham Industries. He plans to detonate the bomb on top of Metro's tallest structure."

It made sense. The fact it was Robert Latham's corporate headquarters made it a bitter irony. Paul rubbed his chin. It was now or never. Everything from here on out had to be executed perfectly. Everything depended on their success.

The possibility of failure was unthinkable.

* * * * * *

Robert Latham sat comfortably in his oversized chair, watching the various news services with rampant eagerness. He was safely tucked away in his secure bunker, located deep beneath his newly rebuilt home. He had plenty of supplies to last him months, perhaps even years, if the need arose. Watching MNN and other channels, he honestly could not discern what the future held for himself or his city. It was of great concern. Perhaps it was time to start thinking bigger, beyond just Metro. The idea lingered briefly before tapering away.

Hmm, he thought, watching the stock market ticker scroll along the bottom of the MNN screen. *My stocks are riding high. At least there's some good news today.*

And, while all hell was breaking loose above ground, down here he finally had some time to rest, as well as remove the prosthetic from his painful stump. Ordinarily, rest would be the last thing on his mind. He was a workaholic, and always had been. The thought of rest, of sleep, was like little slices of death to him. He abhorred it. But today was different. This time it was forced upon him, yes, but it also allowed him the time to think about everything he'd gone through recently.

And perhaps a little rest wasn't always such a bad thing. At least his leg no longer ached. 14

* * * * * *

"There!"

Max, seated at the monitor screen within the Lair, and swiveled in his chair, a broad grin splashed across his face.

"White noise activated?" Paul said, standing some feet across from him.

"Blaring all across the city. If my calculations are right, there should be no more violent incidents within hearing distance of the early warning system."

"We'll just have to hope your calculations are spot on," Paul said, as he turned and began to walk toward the rack of Wraith uniforms hanging along the far wall.

"Will Lady Wraith be joining us tonight?" Max said, now walking alongside Paul.

"No," Paul replied. "And there's no us."

"What?" Max said, obviously incredulous at what he had just heard.

"The housekeeper can't stay here tonight, so we need someone home with Emily and Simpson. And you're in no condition for a night of intense action."

Max's normally cheerful expression turned sour. "Chief, that's about the dumbest thing you've ever said to me. Look at you." He indicated Paul's injured torso and face. "You're hardly in peak condition yourself."

Paul, pulling on his Wraith uniform, made to speak, but Max shut him down quickly.

"And besides, I'm the only person who can disarm that bomb. I constructed it, I can deconstruct it."

Paul placed his cowl over his head. Max's words rung true. It *was* true he had little idea about how to disarm a nuclear device, but he would save everyone if he could, even if it meant sacrificing himself. Of course, if he failed, all would be lost. Clearly, he was exhausted and making little sense.

"You're right, Max, you're right," Paul sighed. "But are you prepared for this? Only you know what you've been through these last few years. I need you ready and primed."

"Let's go, Chief," Max proclaimed. "This city needs us."

The Wraith knew that destiny awaited them this night. He only hoped it would be theirs, not the Cobra's, that would be fulfilled.

* * * * * *

"Here they come again!" a harried voice crackled over Sloan's radio.

Sloan, once again in position at a second-floor window, shook his head with abject resignation. He had hoped the crisis had been averted, but clearly that had been a chimera. "How many?" he barked into his radio.

"Too many," came the reply. "We won't have enough ammunition to hold out much longer."

"The NG unit downstairs manning the barricades is freshly stocked, and can hold the line. Don't fire unless forced to," Sloan said.

"They're a small unit," Perez said, not shifting her gaze from the below street. "Their numbers have been decimated in recent times with what we've had to go through here."

"I know it," Sloan said, perhaps a little sharply, "but they're well-armed and trained. They can give us the time we need."

"For what?"

Sloan took a deep breath. He didn't really know. "A miracle," he finally said.

Gunfire shook him from his thoughts, snapping him back to the immediate situation. He could now see another massive crowd barging toward their building, the same wanton violence in their expressions as before. They were marching to their obliteration, or their own if their dwindling reserves of ammo ran out.

As the NG unit below them fired shot after shot, a sudden cacophonous noise emanated all around them.

"What the hell is that?" Sloan said, reaching for his ears. It was like the whooshing sound you used to hear as the test pattern played on the television late at night. It was disorienting as all heck, that was for sure, Sloan thought.

"Look!" Perez cried out.

"They've stopped marching!" a sniper's voice came through over the radio.

Sloan craned his neck through the window to get a better view. It was true; not only had the crowd stopped in their tracks, but seemed to be shaking their heads in bewilderment. Then they started shaking violently. It was a bizarre and discomfiting sight to behold.

"Hold your fire!" Sloan shouted through the window and repeated into his radio.

He took another look at the crowd. It was as though the entire assemblage, en masse, was having some sort of seizure. Sloan had seen a cousin once having an epileptic fit, and this brought back unpleasant memories of that event. After a few more moments, they all dropped to the ground, seemingly dead to the world.

Wait, Sloan thought. *Did this noise do this? Or was it something else?*

"What was that you said about a miracle?" Perez said, an eyebrow raised.

"It's The Wraith," Sloan whispered. "It has to be. That noise, the crowd stopping. That's no coincidence. But the crowd dropping like flies like that? I'm not sure."

"You might be right," Perez said. "He always has a knack of coming through when he's most needed."

Sloan smiled. He felt sure she was finally starting to see The Wraith in a new light. He knew full well vigilantism was an anathema to her, but The Wraith's results spoke for themselves. The world was never purely black and white. Sloan had long realized a multitude of shades of grey existed in all facets of life.

"We better head out there and check on those people. I can't tell from here if they're alive or dead," Sloan said.

Perez nodded, then said, "That noise isn't letting up. Probably a good thing. If it is acting as you claim, it better keep up its irritating tune."

Perez had a point. He could only hope The Wraith had everything worked out, so that this nightmare would soon cease.

* * * * * *

The Cobra sat cross-legged on a large mat on the floor of another of his secret bolt holes. He was surrounded by members of his elite guard, a series of Blackstorms outfitted like all the others, but these featured black hoods over their heads instead of the pseudo-hockey masks.

His eyes were closed, and he was laser focused on a multitude of internal tasks. He was now so powerful he could control innumerable people throughout the city over great distances. He could shield his various locations from view through sheer force of will, and he could invade the dreams of anyone he chose. He could also meditate at the same time, replenishing his strength at the same time he was expending it.

He also ruminated over his life–his tragedies, triumphs, loves and conquests. All of it had made him the man–the deity–he was today. Remembering his childhood brought him both pain and exhilaration. He recalled the beatings he had withstood, both from his bloated excuse of a father, and the various children in his village, but also felt the joy of taking the ultimate revenge upon them all.

His heart ached for his lost loves–his beloved Persian Leopard, Pashmir, and his woman, Natalya Blackova, who gave herself to him as no other ever had, or ever could. He recalled his faithful servant, Magnus Khan, who he was forced to eliminate recently. And he remembered the infidel, Paul Sanderson, who came into his life at various intervals and proved to be the most annoying of insects, along with his infernal replacement. Their encounter atop that Eritrean mountaintop had altered the trajectory of his life forever, for good and bad. He hated the infidel for denying him his full gift, while reveling in his powers all the same. 15

His eyes suddenly snapped open. Thinking of Sanderson had enraged him, and he had no wish to feel this way. All was proceeding as planned. Soon, the first stage of the fulfillment of his ultimate destiny would be complete. Years of planning, of building his strength, of controlling the course of those around him, were all coming to a head now.

He licked his lips with anticipation. Soon, he would cause unmitigated harm against all those who would oppose him. He would taste the blood of his victims as he conducted the slaughter himself, with his bare hands if necessary. But first, Metro City would be made an example of, to show the world his true power and demonstrate who their one true master was. His hated nemesis, The Wraith, would pay the ultimate price.

That fact alone brought a smile to his face. Then a chuckle. He felt a sense of joy he rarely experienced, and he delighted in it.

"It is time, master," one of the Blackstorms said.

The Cobra nodded and averted his smile. He was enjoying the experience, but he knew he had to hold himself in check. There would be time for exhilaration later. Now it was time to retreat to a safe location, and watch his destiny unfold.

"Phase one will now begin," the Cobra said as he stood.

* * * * * *

The Wraith and Max had planned to arrive at the Latham Industries complex early. They miscalculated. The security screens that were always in place on street level after a certain hour were present, except in the main front entrance. There they had been smashed open. Obviously the Cobra, or his lackeys, had already arrived.

The Wraith and Max rushed inside to find the bodies of staff working late and security guards littering the foyer and hallways leading to the elevators. Death and destruction always lay in the Cobra's wake.

"We're too late," The Wraith said.

"No, we still have time," Max said, as they bolted for the elevators.

Once inside, Max pressed the button for the thirty-second floor, the highest the elevator would take them. Then it was another flight of stairs up to the very top, where the intricate tower was situated on the rooftop. It was there that Max said the bomb would be secreted.

"If only we'd gotten here sooner," The Wraith said.

Max shook his head. "We would have then run the risk of them detonating the bomb earlier, before we could get even a chance at disarming it."

"The Cobra would never risk harm to himself, surely?"

"If he's forced into a corner, I think he would," Max said. "Besides, he has a failsafe escape route in place that–"

The elevator dinged its arrival. The doors opened to reveal three Blackstorms at the far end of the corridor, who differed slightly in appearance from others of their kind. Their masks had been replaced by samples in pitch black, and they stood guard before a closed door leading to the stairs. They showed no sign of surprise or alarm at their presence. The Wraith and Max proceeded cautiously, prepared for anything.

"We were told to expect anything," the Blackstorm standing in the middle said. "This, however, will be a delicious challenge. And a final reckoning for you."

The Wraith replied by activating the Eyes of Judgment on his chest, its fervent energies bathing the corridor in an eerie shade of crackling yellow. "You will be judged for the evil of your actions and the evil in your hearts. And you will be dealt with accordingly."

"Like you have dealt with the others of our kind," the middle Blackstorm said, "we shall deal with you."

It was a challenge that The Wraith and Max were forced to undertake. The Dread Avenger had used up all his flash pellets in his earlier engagement, and Max had not had time to supply or manufacture replacements. This would be a battle of strength, of fortitude, and perhaps a little luck.

The beginning of the end was about to commence.

~ Chapter 10 ~

The future of Metro City, and the world, now came down to this. The Wraith knew they had to prevail. Heaven help them all were they to fail.

They needed an advantage. The Wraith tossed a smoke pellet at the Blackstorms feet, engulfing them all in a thick, charcoal-colored haze. The Wraith was adept at combat in such an environment, and he charged at his foes, letting loose with a battery of forceful blows. It was like smashing a fist into a brick wall. Each punch sent shockwaves through his entire body. He wondered if he was having any impact at all.

"Pitiful fool," a Blackstorm mocked. "We are the master's elite guard. None have ever defeated us in conflict."

One swatted at The Wraith as though he was a fly. The force of the blow sent the Dread Avenger careening back, and wondering if his head was still connected to his neck. He had just managed to roll with the punch ever-so-slightly. It wasn't much, but it was just enough, he thought, that it had saved his life. Even so, his jaw hurt and his ears were ringing.

Max was faring no better than he had, struggling to make any sort of headway against another powerful adversary. Max, getting nowhere fast, retreated back to his friend's side.

"This city will be cleansed from the stench of the infidel," a Blackstorm said. "The master's destiny of conquest will be fulfilled. Nothing can stop this now."

The Wraith's fury upon hearing this knew no bounds. He was injured and fatigued, but none of that mattered now, and his rage fueled him as never before. "This city will never fall to the likes of you. Your time of judgment is now at hand."

Perhaps his speed took his opponents by surprise. Perhaps his rage caught them off guard. Whatever it was, with a cry of anger, this time when his punches hit their marks, the Blackstorms flinched. Not a lot, at first, but it was enough to urge him on. Each punch sent slivers of intense pain through him, like icy-hot tendrils embedded in his nerves. Each punch connected. The Blackstorms fought back valiantly, causing him further injury, but his mind was set on success and he refused to bow down.

One Blackstorm lunged at him and grabbed him in a mighty bear hug, trying to squeeze the life from him. He cried out as he felt sure another rib had snapped.

"Chief!" Max cried. "The Eyes!"

The Wraith reignited the Eyes of Judgment, and the intense burst shot outward, scalding the Blackstorm badly. The concentrated blast forced the villain to stagger back and The Wraith, his jaw clenched, gritted through the pain. He had to end this now. With the Blackstorm still recoiling in agony, he struck again with rights and lefts of incredible strength. This time, the Blackstorm was unable to counter.

The others attempted to counter The Wraith's ascendancy, but he was having none of it. Spinning sidekicks caught them mid-stride, sending them harshly to the floor. He allowed them to stand, but no further opportunity, letting his fists do all the talking. Each of his blows caused more and more pain to his adversaries. Their flinches turned into recoil. The Wraith landed punch after punch, kick after kick. Ultimately, the Blackstorms' speed slowed, their strength clearly slackened. They were hurt and spent.

"You will be judged sorely for your transgressions," The Wraith said, his voice harshened almost to the point of madness. "You spoke of being cleansed and now your souls will burn and be cleansed in due course."

He activated his Eyes of Judgment again, then lashed out at the Blackstorm nearest him, snapping his kneecap with a stomp, then delivering a spinning scissor kick to another, also sending that villain painfully to his knees.

One was left. Even with his cowl, The Wraith could see the fear in the Blackstorm's eyes. The Blackstorm, holding his scalded arms to one side, staggered back in terror. The Wraith advanced. Finally, the villain bumped into the doorway. He turned and seemed to consider scampering up to the roof, but turned and decided to meet his fate with the Dread Avenger of the Underworld.

The Blackstorm snarled and charged at The Wraith, who delivered the roundhouse punch to end all punches, smashing teeth in the process. He joined the other two on the floor.

The Wraith wasn't finished with them yet. He approached them, grabbed the simpering Blackstorm with the shattered knee and yanked him up. "Your soul will burn as you face all the evil you have caused and partaken of. You will be judged accordingly."

He forced this Blackstorm's gaze into the Eyes, and he screamed in abject torment. A few moments longer, he slumped down in a heap. He repeated this with the other two, no longer in any position to stop him, with the same result. The Wraith left the three of them there, writhing in the fetal position. Looking to Max, he made a run for the door.

"I only hope there's time left to disarm the weapon," Max said, bringing up the rear. The stairs were long and steep, but The Wraith vaulted them two at a time. Victory had a renewing effect on him. A few moments later and they were in the open air, the chill of the night greeting them. What also greeted them were another two Blackstorms.

"How many of these goons do we need to take down?" Max muttered.

One was standing guard, while the other was preparing the bomb.

"I know not how you came to pass my brethren below," the Blackstorm on guard said above the wind, "but it matters not. You will not escape. And you will not stop us. The master's destiny will be consummated."

The Eyes of Judgment on The Wraith's chest burst into life once more. He'd had enough of it. "I am getting sick and tired of hearing about your master's *destiny*. Mine is to stop him, and all others who would do harm. You will not halt me, now or ever!"

The Wraith did not allow the Blackstorm to react, and went on the immediate attack, lashing out with a multitude of blows in quick succession. The Blackstorm could do nothing but defend, and even that was failing to prevent him being bombarded with a series of muscular punches and kicks.

"I...I do not...understand," the Blackstorm gasped. "How...is this possible?"

Anger, adrenalin, and a thirst for justice powered The Wraith beyond the limits of mortal man. All life on this planet was potentially down to him in this very moment. He had no capacity for failure.

"Max, the bomb!" The Wraith shouted.

The Irishman grabbed at the remaining Blackstorm, attempted to engage him in combat, to divert his attention from the bomb if nothing else, but the villain would have none of it, sending Max flying with a backward slap.

Max landed in a heap on his rear, and The Wraith caught sight of this out of the corner of his eye. But he dared not let up. The Blackstorm was a most deadly adversary. One slip and all would be lost. He let loose with a powerful punch, sending his opponent down.

In that instant, he reached for his grapnel gun and fired it at the other Blackstorm, who had returned to the device. The hook slammed into the back of his shoulder, puncturing it, and blood spurted from the wound. The Blackstorm cried out in pain, and The Wraith yanked hard on the line, bringing the villain racing toward him. He delivered a roundhouse punch to the jaw, sending the Blackstorm to sleep.

The sole Blackstorm was now up on his knees. There was little defiance left in him. The Wraith's rage had taken its toll.

"This cannot be," Blackstorm said. "Nobody has ever bested me in combat."

The Wraith snorted. "I keep hearing that lately. And yet here we are."

"I cannot brook this humiliation," the Blackstorm said, as he crunched down on something hard and began to gurgle. "The bomb is set and nothing can stop it now..."

The Blackstorm fell down dead. It was clear he'd taken his own life with a poison secreted within his mouth.

Lady Wraith suddenly dropped down beside them, replacing her grapnel gun into her belt. "I missed all the action."

"Quickly, Max," The Wraith directed, briefly ignoring her. "Disarm that thing."

Max saluted and started to work.

"What about Emily?" The Wraith said.

"The housemaid returned, said everything was going crazy out there, and she came quickly back. With Emily and Simpson now being looked after, I couldn't just stand back and let you face all this by yourselves."

The Wraith smiled weakly and placed a comforting hand on her shoulder. Their work was over for the time being. Now it was down to Max.

The Irishman produced a set of tools from his belt and started dismantling the surrounding sphere, separating it into two halves. The Wraith and Lady Wraith stood behind him, the former spotting the digital countdown.

"We have plenty of time if that display is accurate," The Wraith said, noting they had three hours remaining before detonation.

Max did not reply, as he started to remove a small, cylindrical tin from one of the halves with extreme caution.

"Is that it?" Lady Wraith said. "It's so small."

"It doesn't take much of this stuff to cause a helluva lot of damage," Max said in a hushed tone.

"Is it...I mean...are we...?" Lady Wraith said, no doubt worrying about radiation exposure.

"This is lead-lined, if that's what you mean," Max replied.

Lady Wraith took in a sharp breath. Max removed the cylinder from its housing, and then all hell broke loose. The countdown began racing. Lady Wraith gasped.

"Oh no," Max said in desperation, "I'd forgotten about the trick switch I installed."

He fiddled frantically with the various intricate wires attaching the cylinder to the main housing, but the countdown still raced. He snipped one wire, then another, and the countdown slowed to its normal pace, but it was still counting down.

The Wraith's eyes bulged open. There were only just over sixty seconds remaining. The Dread Avenger's mouth was dry, his throat felt constricted, and his heart pounded. "Max...is there enough time?"

The Irishman didn't reply, but worked feverishly, pulling on a circuit, flicking a switch, and snipping another wire or two. The Wraith could make no sense of it.

Fifty seconds remaining became forty-five, then forty. Still the display counted down. And Max continued working.

"Hurry!" Lady Wraith said frantically, as the counter reached thirty seconds.

Sweat was running down The Wraith's chin. He wiped it away as best he could.

"That's not helping," Max muttered, not stopping his work for an instant.

Twenty-five, twenty, fifteen. Max was still fiddling.

"Max!"

Ten seconds. Nine, eight, seven.

The Wraith felt as though time had almost come to a halt. Everything was moving in slow motion.

Six, five, four.

"Aha!" Max proclaimed, and he flicked one last switch.

The display read two seconds remaining, but it no longer moved.

The Wraith held his breath, not sure whether it was all truly over. Lady Wraith was almost in tears.

"It was harder than I thought," Max said with a smile, in surprisingly better shape than the others. "Kind of like a doctor struggling to read their own hand writing. My work proved more intricate than I remembered."

The Wraith finally took in a deep breath. "You did it, Max."

"Thank goodness," Lady Wraith breathed.

The Wraith's mind was racing. Their task was not yet finished. The Cobra remained at large, and while he did so, all was still at risk.

"We've at last gained the upper hand," The Wraith said. "The Cobra will undoubtedly not have anticipated we would disarm the weapon. So, we have a few hours to play with here."

"Not really," Max said, putting a dampener on proceedings. "The Cobra will need time to make his escape, to put enough miles behind him to be safe from the blast."

"That means..." Lady Wraith began.

"Yes," Max said. "The Cobra will be leaving any moment now."

~ Chapter 11 ~

Sloan reached for another pulse. Again, nothing. So far, all appeared deceased. Dozens of people had just dropped dead for no apparent reason. He pushed a hand through his thinning hair. He doubted their deaths were because of the noise, which still had not abated, but he couldn't tell for sure. All this was way above his pay grade.

"What do you think?" Perez said, eyeing her partner trudging through the morass of corpses.

"Apart from the fact that they're dead?" Sloan asked. "I don't know."

Armed cops patrolled all around, on high alert, ready in case more zombies appeared.

"You think this racket caused all this?" Perez said.

"I doubt it," Sloan replied, "but I'm in no position to say."

She crouched down, and Sloan could tell she was trying to gather her thoughts.

"Either way, whatever caused this saved our lives and the rest of the city," she said.

"What's left of it," Sloan said, feeling weary beyond belief.

He felt grateful, too, just as Perez clearly did, but he also felt guilty, angry, frustrated, and awash with pretty much every other emotion. It was too much for him to make any sense of right now. It would take time to work through it. He wondered if he'd ever be the same again.

"I can see you're troubled," she said, coming up to her partner. "I'm in the same boat. We did all we could, the best way we knew how. I don't think we could have made any other decisions under the circumstances."

"I know, I know," he said. "You're right, but knowing this doesn't make much difference to me." He pushed a hand through his hair again. "I'll work through this, somehow. I always do."

He put his arm around her and gave her a bit of a hug. He knew he would be all right, given time and a little loving care from his wife. Perhaps now *was* the time for that long promised vacation. He made a vow to himself to sort that out once this was over.

"Let's head back inside," he said. "I'll leave a small batch of men out to keep watch, but I don't think those zombies will trouble us again. We have to report in and..." he sighed, "...we have a funeral to arrange."

* * * * * *

The Cobra strode toward his aircraft, an old, stripped down B-24, parked in a field on a farmland airstrip. On either side, Blackstorms lined the way, giving him an almost military send-off. Another few moments and they would all be onboard and airborne, flying to safety. Metro City was doomed.

"You will not escape me, Abdelkrim!" The Wraith said, stepping forth from around the plane.

Lady Wraith and Max Horton quickly joined him.

"You are too late," the Cobra mocked. "Your city is doomed. Nothing can save your precious people now."

"You underestimate me again, but then you have a history of that. Don't you recognize Max here beside me? What he can create, he can also demolish."

The Cobra realized the bomb had been defused or destroyed. Either way, his destiny had been derailed yet again. Madness welled inside him. Only spilled blood would quell his thirst now.

"You will pay for every indignity you have brought upon me," the Cobra roared. "I will tear you apart limb-from-limb."

The battle was about to commence. The Cobra would wreak havoc upon his enemies, and all others who dared oppose him.

* * * * * *

"Now!" The Wraith shouted.

Lady Wraith and Max sprinted away from the scene, as The Wraith tossed some explosives from his belt into the rear of the plane. He followed his comrades and, before the Cobra's men knew what was happening, the plane erupted in a gigantic ball of flames. The Wraith, nearest the blast, took the brunt of the explosive force, and was propelled through the air to land harshly in the dirt. His ribs stung, but he was otherwise unharmed as his suit had protected him.

He turned to witness the carnage he had wrought. It appeared the detonation had taken out most of the Blackstorms; some were flailing about ablaze, while others lay unconscious or dead. There was no sign of the Cobra.

"Darling, are you all right?" Lady Wraith said, appearing by The Wraith's side.

"A little bruised but otherwise okay," he said, looking up to her then at Max.

"There'll be no escape for the Cobra now," Max said, whistling at the sight of the nearby inferno.

"The irony is," a familiar, harsh voice spoke, "that there will be no escape for you."

The trio whirled to come face-to-face with the Cobra, a Blackstorm on either side of him. They were all that was left of the Cobra's evil empire. The Wraith vowed in that moment it would end tonight. The Cobra's reign of terror would not be allowed to continue. With three against three, the fate of the world was hanging in the balance.

"This ends now," The Wraith said, his Eyes of Judgment bursting into life.

"You are right," the Cobra said. "With your slaughter!"

The two Blackstorms lurched forward, going immediately on the attack. One took a massive swipe at Max, sending him flying, then turned his attention toward Lady Wraith, briefly catching her off guard. He connected with a couple of punches that caused her to stagger back in pain. The other Blackstorm confronted The Wraith, attempting a blitzkrieg attack of his own.

"You will pay dearly for defying the master," the Blackstorm said, and let loose with a barrage of blows.

The Wraith attempted to block as many of them as possible, but the Blackstorm appeared faster and stronger than the others, or he was beginning to falter. Either way, he was struggling to hold his own.

"You will not survive," the Cobra said, watching on from behind. "My elite guard will take care of you, and I will then deliver the coup de grâce myself."

"You coward," The Wraith grunted, taking another hit. "You have others fight your battles for you."

"Your barbs have no effect on me," the Cobra said. "I will be the victor. Nothing will stand in my way."

The battle raged on. Lady Wraith finally got a few blows in but they proved ineffective. The Blackstorm continued his vicious assault on her, impacting again and again. The Wraith was unable to assist, battling just a short distance away. As he got a kick in to the torso of his enemy, he heard a sickening crack and Lady Wraith screamed.

She was down on her knees in the dust, holding her floppy arm aloft. The Blackstorm had snapped the ulna in two and he clearly wasn't about to leave it there as he was advancing upon her with haste.

"Fry!" The Wraith cried.

Lady Wraith, tears streaming down her face, struggled to reach the relevant button on her belt, but did so with not a moment to spare. Her Eyes of Judgment blared into intense life, vaporizing her antagonist in a burst of energy. She then fell into unconsciousness. 16

The Cobra growled in anger and the incident caused the remaining Blackstorm to pause. It was enough for The Wraith to strike with pinpoint blows to the face and throat. The Blackstorm stumbled back in pain, and The Wraith took his chance, striking with a spinning scissor kick to the head. The blow was strong enough to tear the mask from the villain's head and knock him out cold. The battle was over.

The Cobra grumbled with vengeance and his eyes filled with a cold fury The Wraith knew well. "Enough! I will pick the flesh from your bones and drink your blood!"

The villain marched toward The Wraith, and the two traded blows. The Cobra was immensely strong, unlike anyone The Wraith had ever faced. He held his own for the present, but he knew he couldn't keep it up for long. His strength was, indeed, faltering, and his stamina fading. He'd pushed himself beyond all human endurance. He had finally hit the wall. He tried willing his body to push on ever more but it was no good. He had nothing left to give.

"You will beg me to stop, to end your life," the Cobra spat, "but I will prolong your insipid existence long enough to see me slaughter everything you hold dear before I finally show you mercy in death."

The Wraith could do nothing but take hit after hit, kick after kick.

Leena...Emily...

It was over. All was lost.

The Cobra now had him in a mighty headlock, hands positioned around his neck, ready to deliver the killer strike. It was only a matter of moments.

"Now I will rid myself of this most annoying gnat," the Cobra grunted.

Almost on instinct, and with barely any strength remaining, The Wraith plunged a heel down into the Cobra's foot with just enough force to loosen the villain's grip on him. It barely delayed the inevitable, for the Cobra then latched onto his enemy, grabbing him in a powerful bear hug, squeezing the very life from him with apparent ease. Another few moments and it would be over.

At that moment, the Eyes of Judgment involuntarily flared up, shining brighter than ever before. It was enough to shock the Cobra back on his heels, and The Wraith to open his swollen eyes as best he could.

What is...happening...here...?

Darkness was beckoning, ready to claim him forever, but the magnitude of his Judgment Stare, the power emanating from it, was somehow keeping him conscious. And keeping him alive.

The Cobra, screaming, let loose with the force from his right eye, in an apparent attempt to counter the energy from the Eyes. Both their powers originated from the same mystical source in Eritrea. When The Wraith had first received his abilities, it had somehow also birthed the Cobra's in a way he had never fully understood. No matter the truth of it, they were, inexplicably, two sides of the same coin, the Yin to the other's Yang.

It was as much a struggle of wills as of physical strength, as the force from the Eyes began to inch forward, gaining ground, then falling back under the bombardment from the Cobra. It continued thus, back and forth, for a long time, neither side willing to give in. The Wraith, even with his vision strained, could see the gray in the Cobra's temples growing larger with each passing second. It was as though the intense effort being expended was aging him, eating him alive.

The Cobra shrieked with a rage never-before-seen, and he appeared to be, at last, winning the battle of wills between them. "I will grind you into the dust," he grunted through gritted teeth.

It is over...I have nothing left...

Suddenly, from nowhere, a vision of the old man of Emba Soira appeared in a haze above The Wraith.

"What is this trick?" the Cobra hissed.

"You are an abomination," the old man said, "and your existence should never have occurred."

"You speak gibberish," the Cobra snorted. "My destiny has long been foretold. Of power, of conquest over all life."

"You mistake destiny with egoism. *You* are the mistake, one which shall now be finally rectified."

The Wraith, barely able to comprehend what was happening, felt the Eyes of Judgment power up further, beyond anything he had produced himself. The energy bursting forth was beginning to cause him pain, then intensified to an agony he had never experienced or imagined. He screamed. The Cobra screamed, too, as the fiery energies from the Eyes of Judgment overpowered him. They enveloped him and then consumed him in a concentrated ball of flame, as the old man watched on in silence.

The Wraith averted his eyes and held an arm up to protect his vision. There was one last scream from the Cobra, and it was all over. The Judgment Stare ceased as suddenly as it had started. The Wraith lowered his arm and saw what remained of his great enemy–a burned out husk that crumbled into dust under its own weight.

The Wraith coughed and crumbled to his knees. He pulled his cowl off, and coughed again. The conflict had been too much for him. The energy expended to defeat the Cobra had used up everything he had. His soul-force was depleted. In truth, he was mortally wounded, and he knew it. He was dying.

"Without realizing it," the old man said in a whisper, "his destiny *has* been fulfilled. The order of things has been restored." And he vanished softly from view with no explanation.

Paul smiled. It had taken all he had. He hated leaving Leena and Emily all alone. He had so much more to live for, but if this *was* the end, as he knew it to be, saving them and everyone else was worth it. He could ask for nothing more.

"Paul!" Lady Wraith screamed.

She rushed over to his side, despite her own horrific injuries, gently stroked his cheek.

"It is finished," he said, closing his eyes.

He sagged to the ground, blackness embracing him.

* * * * * *

"Nooooooo!" Lady Wraith screeched in abject torment, tears flowing in mighty torrents down her cheeks as she tried to cradle the body of her fiancé in her arms.

"Hold your tears," a gentle voice said. A vision of a tiny, wizened old man, appeared beside them. He was smiling. "All is not yet lost."

"Who are you?" Lady Wraith stammered.

"I am the one this man sought many years and two generations ago," the old man said softly. "I was once the keeper of the power of the Eyes of Judgment, ready and willing to impart them upon the chosen one, one who was deserving of them."

The old man of Eritrea, Lady Wraith thought. *Where Paul–the original Paul–received his powers.*

"But...but how can...?"

"Speak not, my child," the old man said. "Only listen. I passed from this realm before I could fully explain all to the chosen one. He–they–have done their best under trying circumstances. They have done well. By sacrificing himself for the greater good–indeed, in saving all of humanity–Paul Sanderson, has been deemed worthy of the greatest gift of all: immortality."

Lady Wraith's eyes bulged open. She couldn't believe what she was hearing. It was too much for her, and it almost made her forget the intense pain in her right arm.

"So...rise, Paul Sanderson. Rise and live again." The old man reached down, placed a hand on Paul's chest, and instantly he sat bolt upright with a sharp intake of breath, the swelling in his face receding, all his wounds healing in seconds.

"Paul," Lady Wraith spluttered, "you're alive."

He smiled and took her in his arms, the vision of the old man smiling at their side.

"You can still be injured, still become ill," the old man explained. "And your immortality can be removed at a moment of your choosing, when you pass your powers and memories to another. Then you will be as before. But until then...live on, always seeking justice for those who need it, and always putting the greater good above all else. Goodbye, my child. You will hear from me no more."

The vision faded, his smiling face still evident.

"Wait!" Paul said. "I still have so many questions."

Another smile and he was gone for all time. Again, as in Eritrea, leaving so much left unsaid.

A cold wind picked up and, even though it was still night, the sky seemed to darken somehow, as though something was lost.

Something that could never be replaced.

~ Epilogue ~

ONE MONTH LATER

The city was starting to return to a faint semblance of normalcy. After what had recently happened, what could ever be described as normal now? And could the city, and its survivors, ever find peace and solace after all that had occurred? Sloan wondered at that. Thousands had lost their lives in such a senseless orgy of hostility. He wondered if he could ever forgive himself. No matter what, he knew that he could go on, put his anguish into a corner of his mind secure enough to continue to function and do his job, but the pain in his soul would be something he would have to live with for the rest of his life.

Possibly it's better this way, he thought. The moment he felt nothing at all, it was all over. That notion allowed him to go on.

It was a dark and dreary day, overcast and blustery, perhaps fitting under the circumstances. Sloan, Perez, and their fellow officers were outfitted in regimental dress, and had congregated on the city's main street, sitting atop a dais. Mayor Hutchison was standing in front of them. Behind them were placards featuring Commissioner Harrison's face.

Without his toupée, Sloan chuckled inwardly. *He wouldn't have liked that.*

This was both a memorial service for the slain commissioner and something else, to be conducted at the conclusion of the commissioner's service.

"We are all gathered here today to celebrate the life of a man who was one of the best of us," Mayor Hutchison spoke into the microphone. "Commissioner George Harrison rose from the ranks to reach the highest office in his profession because of his work ethic, his hard-headedness, and his integrity. In a city long renowned for its corruption, Harrison came along and cleaned the place up through sheer force of will. We will all be forever grateful to him for that."

Sloan, seated behind the standing mayor, looked down toward the crowd. Those surrounding the decorated coffin of his dearly departed boss and friend were mostly cops. There was a small crowd of civilians, some from the business community, others just wishing to pay their last respects at a service open to the public. Beside him on the dais sat Perez–at Sloan's insistence–while the rest of the dais was filled with Harrison's grieving family, various local dignitaries, and a man he despised, Robert Latham.

"This city stands today because of Commissioner Harrison's commitment and courage to do what was right, no matter the cost. Sadly, this time that cost was almost too great, losing his life in the defense of this city, and its people," Hutchison extolled. "But the truth is, and Harrison well knew this, no cost is too great when Metro City is at stake. Harrison died to save others. He died a hero, and we will never forget him and will forever honor him."

Hutchison lifted his arms in tribute, and everyone in the crowd cheered at the top of their lungs. Those immediately surrounding the coffin lifted their rifles, pointed them upwards, and fired a series of shots in unison. Sloan looked over to his partner. She had tears in her eyes. He handed her his handkerchief. She sniffed into it. He knew how she felt. He felt it, too. He'd come up with Harrison in the service, after all. They'd each shared a lifetime of triumphs and tragedies together. Both were incorruptible with a resolute sense of justice and propriety. It was the portion of the ceremony that was still to come that, somehow, seemed out of place to him, but the matter was out of his hands.

"As we commemorate our fallen friend, we must also fulfill a solemn duty, one which I know Commissioner Harrison would be smiling down upon us about. Please stand, Detective Robert Sloan."

Sloan did so, and reluctantly took the few steps toward the mayor. He hated such pageantry. The crowd erupted in claps and cheers.

"This medal for bravery," Hutchison said, pinning it to Sloan's tunic, "is a symbol of all that is good in our city, and all that you have achieved on our behalf. Because of you, and those others in the force under your voluntary command, countless lives were saved. We salute you, Commissioner Sloan."

A chorus of cheers, whistles, claps, and hoots exploded amongst those congregated. Sloan smiled weakly. He would have preferred all this done in private, with the focus on Harrison alone and his heroic sacrifice, but he'd had little say in the matter. Hutchison was always one for the dramatic, and even in their collective grief, the mayor wanted to put on something of a show. And now he had to make a speech, which he'd always hated doing. It would be brief.

"Thank you, Mayor Hutchison, Mr. Latham, fellow dignitaries, ladies, and gentlemen," Sloan began. "I wouldn't be here today without Commissioner Harrison. He saved my life, literally and otherwise, countless times. He wasn't just my boss. He was my friend. I trusted him as I do very few others in life, save my wife, and also my partner, Rosa Perez." He indicated to his wife, Janet at the front of the crowd, and to his partner seated behind him. "I would have preferred today be solely about my friend, but...so be it. I thank you for this great honor, and I promise you all...I won't let you down." He waved at the cheering crowd. "Thank you."

He returned to his seat and zoned out the rest of the ceremony. He turned to Perez. "I never thought I'd ever rise above detective and even reaching that was because Harrison believed in me and lifted me up when I needed a kick in the ass."

"You deserve this honor, Bob," she said, her eyes glistening. "There is no finer choice for commissioner. It's just that..."

"What?" he said, confused. Then, it hit him just as Perez spoke again.

"We won't be partners anymore," she sniffed, looking a little embarrassed, no doubt the significance of the occasion getting to her. "I'm not sure how I feel about that."

"Nothing much will change, I promise you. We'll still be working hand-in-glove, as always," Sloan said. "I'll only be down the hall from you."

She smiled weakly and nodded at him. He wasn't sure that was enough for her. She would soon be assigned a new partner, after all, but he knew she'd guts it out as she always did. As she always would.

"Come on, Perez," Sloan said. "Do you mind helping me back at the station?"

She smiled.

He knew it was best to keep busy when one was in pain. Time and work helped heal all wounds.

He could only hope this time would be no different.

* * * * * *

Robert Latham arrived back at his rebuilt estate after the various ceremonial duties had been completed. He stepped gingerly from his limo and looked up at the new house he had built to replace his previous home.

It was a state-of-the-art abode, built to survive all forms of natural disaster, and as strong as a fortress to prevent any such intrusions that had occurred in the past. It was more modern in style, architecturally speaking, than his previous home, but as with his newly designed office at Latham Industries, he somehow felt this was indicative of his rebirth. The world had changed irrevocably, and he needed to change along with it. Or he would be left mouldering in the dust along with other monuments.

His thoughts then turned to what the future might hold, and how tenuous his hold on life really was, and anyone else's. He wondered briefly if his hold on the city would or could be maintained long term. Beings of such power, like the Cobra, were beyond his ken. Anything they did, and the atrocities they committed, was out of his control. And yet...

"Is anything the matter, sir?" his driver Smithers enquired.

"Hmm? Oh no. I am just thinking of things. Of the past. Of the future."

Smithers raised an eyebrow at that, clearly not understanding what Latham had said. "Very good, sir."

Latham sniffed. Smithers didn't understand, nor cared, about any of that. He briefly envied his chauffeur for it.

"Park the car in its usual spot, Smithers. I won't be needing you for the rest of the day."

Latham would be working from home. He had ideas he wished to pursue, but they had to foment in his mind first.

All would come to pass in time.

* * * * * *

The clouds cleared in the early afternoon, and Paul, Leena, Max, and Emily emerged from Sanderson House and walked into their expansive front garden, the little blonde girl leading the way with a hop and a skip. Most of the fenced property was in front of the house, with a lengthy driveway and a plethora of well-kept foliage. Poplar, oak, and elm trees dotted the grounds, their leaves scattered on the lawn, and there were a variety of flowering shrubs, some that bloomed throughout the year.

In amongst the huge grassed lawn, the family had recently installed a playground, complete with swings, slide, and a climbing rig, amongst other equipment. It was toward this that Emily now headed. Leena helped the little girl into the swing and started her pendulum going.

"I can do it myself," Emily said, and she did, crying out in sheer joy, laughing, and hooting.

Leena took a few steps over to Max and both watched the girl enjoying herself in the sunshine. Then Max turned to check on Paul, who was seated in a nearby lawn chair, his expression vacant, as though he was a returned war veteran suffering from shell-shock.

"The Chief looks sort of dead inside," Max said, his face furrowed with great concern.

"He's been this way ever since that night," Leena said. "He feels guilty about what we were forced to do. He blames himself for the death of all those people. It's almost as if he wished himself dead again."

"Survivor's guilt?" Max said.

"In a way," Leena said. "As he lay there dying, I think...I think he felt that his death had somehow atoned for his perceived sins. But now..."

Max shook his head. "He mustn't feel that way. As soon as the Cobra controlled all those people, their fate was sealed."

Leena's eyes opened in shock. "What did you just say?"

"I've been doing some research. The white noise broke the Cobra's mental control over the people, as I surmised, but once freed from their imprisonment, their brains were so damaged they all fell down dead."

"So," Leena uttered, "you mean...?"

"Yes," Max said, "they were dead already. The Cobra had fried their brains. Nothing we did made any real difference to them. We didn't murder anyone. Only the Cobra can claim credit for that."

Leena turned to Paul. She would tell him later, and they would inform Sloan of their findings. It would make a difference. But she had no idea how he was dealing with his new life status, or how he would in the future.

She only hoped Max's revelation would help.

* * * * * *

Paul was both cognizant of his surrounds, and what was happening around him, and dead to the world at the same time. It was an odd sensation, but he really didn't know how to break free of his torpor. They had won, and saved millions of lives, but at what cost?

"Daddy," Emily said, bounding up to Paul in his chair, "will you please play with me?"

Tears flooded Paul's eyes, and they fell in streams down his face. He smiled and took the little girl in his arms, embracing her with all the love in his heart. He lifted her up and held her close. "I would love to play with you."

"Come on then, Daddy," she said, "follow me." And she led the way further into the garden, Paul following close behind, with Leena bringing up the rear.

They would be all right because they were a family, and they had each other. Love would always conquer all.

~ Author's Note ~

This story really is the culmination of all I had planned for this series. When I started it, crime lord Robert Latham was always intended as the central villain, the so-called spider within the city's web of evil, who would feature throughout in just about every volume, either as the central antagonist, or in some sort of supporting role. And, this has proven to be the case. The Cobra, however, was intended to be The Wraith's ultimate villain. Think of Latham as The Wraith's Lex Luthor, then the Cobra becomes his General Zod. Powerful, with past connections, their lives and powers intertwined in mysterious and sinister ways.

Ever since the debut novel in the series, *The Wraith*, I had been planning for the Cobra's return, and laid clues and developed subplots along the way hinting at this eventuality. Some subtle, some less so. Most volumes in the series featured at least one hint, one clue, to the villain's eventual return. I'm proud to have developed such an entwined narrative over the course of the last two decades. And now here we are. I hope that pay off was worth it. While I can never be sure of the success of my own endeavors, I am overall satisfied with the results.

There is something of a new status quo with the end of this novel, and it sort of serves as a new jumping-off point for the rest of the series. Trust me, the adventures of The Wraith will go on, and I have many more tales to tell, starting with the next in the series, *Birds of the Living Dead*. This is another story that has been long in the offing, and I can't wait to release it for your reading pleasure.

Also in the pipeline is Book Three in the *Books of Judgment* sub-series, *Rising Son*, which will be co-written with my valued colleague, Adam Oravec (who co-wrote the fantastic *Lady Wraith* with me). This will be the never-before-seen origin of Robert Latham. How he started with absolutely nothing, to become the most powerful and ruthless figure on the American east coast. A thrilling, powerful crime saga, coming to you sometime in 2026.

As always, there are people I'd like to thank before signing off. My family, who are always there for me, get the ultimate thanks. I am nothing without them. Thanks also to my editors, AP Fuchs and Joanne Lane. They both did a superb job with this book, honing it to perfection. And thanks to you, once again, my dear readers. I do all this for you. Ultimately, it's *all* for you. Thank you.

2025 has been a banner year for The Wraith and Glowing Eyes Media. As of this writing, four volumes in the series have been released thus far (*Swamp Witch of Satan's Forest, Lady Wraith, Kingdom* and this book currently in your hands), with *Birds of the Living Dead* and *The Acolyte* coming closer to the end of the year (with several volumes coming in 2026). I'm proud to have been able to make up for some lost time while looking after my infant daughter at home, and I hope you have enjoyed this book and all those others mentioned. Time to get back to my writing desk. I'll see you in the next one.

Take care.

Frank Dirscherl
Wollongong, 2025

~ Explanatory Notes ~

Because this book has come so many years since the first in the series (and the last time the villainous Cobra appeared in this main series), I thought it best to add some explanatory notes for this book (purely as a one-off). I'm sure you noticed the various numbers sprinkled throughout the book, and here are the explanations for those. Enjoy.

1. The Cobra's real name, Abdelkrim, was first revealed in the Books of Judgment Book Two, *Serpent Rising*, and then in the reprint editions of the first book in the main series, *The Wraith*.

2. Natalya Blackova's first appearance in the first two books in the series, *The Wraith* and *Valley of Evil* and appeared to perish in the latter. Her origin was addressed in the Cobra's origin story, *Serpent Rising*, and her survival was confirmed in #7 in the series, *Vendetta*. She is now on the side of good, operates under the moniker the Siren, and is a founding member of the Global Protectors (appearing in a future novel). The Cobra is unaware of her survival.

3. Magnus Khan was the Cobra's loyal lieutenant. He appeared in *The Wraith* and *Valley of Evil*, being incarcerated in a lunatic asylum at the end of the latter. He also appeared in *Serpent Rising*, where the Cobra brutally assassinated him.

4. There has been a downcast, depressing mood permeating through Metro City ever since *Valley of Evil*, a running subplot in most of the books in the series since then. That was the Cobra's mental influence over the city's people during that time.

5. That's right. The Cobra infiltrated Sanderson House during *Cry of the Werewolf* and Max has been in the villain's unconscious thrall ever since.

6. Emma Sanderson first appeared in *Lady Wraith*, and was adopted by Paul and Leena in the following book, *Kingdom*.

7. Perez is referring to the events of *Lady Wraith* and *Kingdom*, where Sloan was put through the wringer, along with the rest of Metro City.

8. Blackstorm was revealed as a key member of the Cobra's staff in *Lady Wraith*. And at least one of their brethren has appeared since then.

9. Fatback aka Fatty was introduced in *Lady Wraith* as a stoolie of indeterminate occupation.

10. John Carruthers became Robert Latham's right-hand man in Kingdom. Smithers has been Latham's longtime chauffeur.

11. The Christopher Docks feature prominently in many of the books in the series.

12. Dr. Needham has long been Paul's personal physician, a fact established in the very first book, *The Wraith*.

13. This is in reference to the original Paul Sanderson's journey to the country, and where he was endowed with his powers, in *Sanderson of Metro*.

14. Latham lost his leg in *Vendetta*, an injury sustained when Crossfire tried to kill him in his home.

15. Some/all of these events in the Cobra's life are referenced in both *Sanderson of Metro* and *Serpent Rising*.

16. Leena's first appearance as Lady Wraith was in *Vendetta*, also the first time her suit and its abilities were explained by Max.

Art by Michael DiPascale

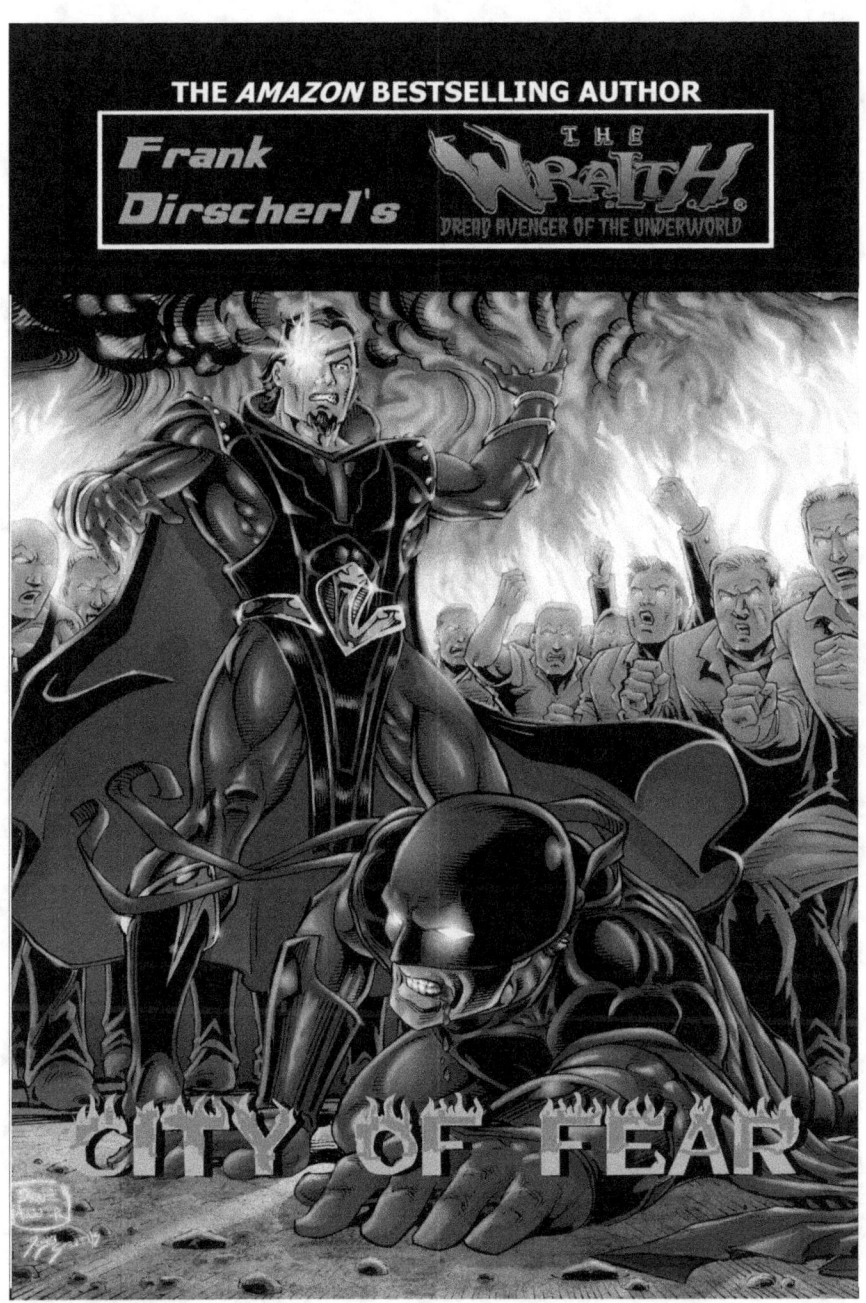

Art by Dave Hoover and Doug Stevens

BIRDS OF THE LIVING DEAD

~ Sneak peek ~

Here is a special sneak peek at the following novel in the series, *Birds of the Living Dead*. Please enjoy chapter 1 of this exciting book...

~ Prologue ~

"I now pronounce you husband and wife."

Paul Sanderson was resplendent in a bespoke tailored wedding suit from his tailors at Cad and the Dandy, and his now wife, Leena, looked gorgeous in her ivory white gown from Allure–her gently curled strawberry blonde hair cascading down. As they kissed, the entire cathedral erupted in a cacophony of cheers and joy.

They turned to face the large crowd congregated behind them. Their six-year-old-girl, Emily Roseanne Sanderson, came bounding toward them. She latched onto Paul's leg and gave it a loving squeeze. Simpson sat in the front pew alongside several of the household staff, a smile never leaving his face. He could also see his old friend, Commissioner Bob Sloan, and others from the force, in the pew behind. Even his despised nemesis, Robert Latham, had made an appearance, deigning to appear in public in something other than the city's restoration efforts.

"Well," Max Horton said, Paul's right-hand and best man for the occasion. "It's time to leave."

Paul nodded, took his wife's hand, and they slowly made their way back down the aisle.

"Where are we going again?" Emily asked, adorable in her bridesmaid's dress.

"Our honeymoon," Leena replied. "The Great Barrier Reef in Australia."

"I am coming with you, right?" the little girl asked hesitantly.

"Of course, sweetie," Paul said, crouching down to face his daughter. "We would not go without you."

She smiled and gave Paul the best hug ever. He picked her up and carried her in one hand, holding Leena's in the other. Everyone was smiling, and the cheers continued as they walked slowly forward. Paul thought the cathedral had never looked finer. Its history and architecture had always appealed to Leena and him, and it was beautifully decorated with flowers and colorful lace banners.

Sloan gave Paul a wink as they passed, and even Latham, a dour man since losing his leg, appeared more cheerful than usual and had actually put on a little weight since Paul had seen him last.

Eventually, after giving thanks to a plethora of people, the three of them reached the open air and found their classic Daimler parked out front, adorned with flowers and streamers and stringed cans at its rear. Paul pointed the cans out to his new bride.

"Oh, that's Max all right," she said.

"Did I hear my name?" the Irishman said, bounding up behind them.

Leena smiled. "Are you ready?"

"Airport, here we come," Max said.

He took hold of Emily's hand, secured her in car's rear seats, then scampered around and hopped behind the wheel.

Paul brought Leena in close. "Finally, husband and wife."

"I thought we'd never get here," Leena said, nuzzling him.

"Two weeks away with my family. Heaven." Then a thought came to him. "What about the city?"

"Don't worry," Leena said, an eyebrow raised. "Starflame will keep an eye out on Metro while we're gone. I think we can allow ourselves a little break."

Paul knew his friend and fellow Global Protectors member would do a fine job in their absence. He had to let go and allow himself to enjoy their time away together. His family deserved that. He deserved that.

He escorted his bride over to the car and assisted her inside, then turned and waved to the crowd atop the cathedral steps. He then got in beside Leena and they were left.

~ Also Available ~

The Wraith Dread Avenger of the Underworld #3
CROSSFIRE
Stephen J. Semones & Frank Dirscherl

After a terrorist attack leaves the citizens of Metro City reeling, an enigmatic stranger emerges from the wake of the destruction to wage war on local crime-lord Robert Latham. In the midst of this, Max Horton, The Wraith's right-hand man, vanishes without a trace. Searching for Max, and for those responsible for the devastation, The Wraith sets out for answers.

NOW AVAILABLE!

www.glowingeyesmedia.com

The Wraith Dread Avenger of the Underworld #4
CULT OF THE DAMNED
Frank Dirscherl

With the city back firmly in his grasp, crime lord and entrepreneur Robert Latham is celebrating by bankrolling Metro City's 200th anniversary gala year, which includes the unveiling of a never-before-seen ancient Aztec stone carving—the Cortes Stone—at the City Gallery, a carving that has thrilled the scientific and artistic communities, but infuriated the monstrous Aztekoth.

NOW AVAILABLE!

www.glowingeyesmedia.com

The Wraith Dread Avenger of the Underworld #5
CRY OF THE WEREWOLF
Frank Dirscherl

Having gone through ordeal after ordeal, Paul Sanderson (aka The Wraith Dread Avenger of the Underworld ®) and his love Leena Patterson, decide to take a long overdue vacation. However, their idyll is soon shattered by an attack by a creature nobody thought could possibly exist—a werewolf. Soon, an evil so heinous makes himself known, and only The Wraith could possibly defeat it.

NOW AVAILABLE!

www.glowingeyesmedia.com

The Wraith Dread Avenger of the Underworld #6
SWAMP WITCH OF SATAN'S FOREST

Frank Dirscherl & Ray MacKay

On their way home from their mountain vacation which was anything but, Paul Sanderson (aka The Wraith) and his love Leena Patterson are waylaid by a mysterious cry for help, and are unwittingly drawn into the forest—and the web—of the alluring Swamp Witch.

NOW AVAILABLE!

www.glowingeyesmedia.com

The Wraith Dread Avenger of the Underworld #7
VENDETTA
Frank Dirscherl

After having been betrayed by crime lord, Robert Latham, and
defeated by The Wraith, Crossfire has returned to cause mayhem
and carnage at every turn. His ultimate aim? The utter destruction
of all his enemies, and he doesn't care who gets in his way.

NOW AVAILABLE!

www.glowingeyesmedia.com

The Wraith Dread Avenger of the Underworld #9
KINGDOM
Frank Dirscherl

Crime lord, Robert Latham has returned, seemingly from the dead,
ready to reclaim his kingdom. Ready to take whatever steps are
necessary to restock and rebuild, to recover his rightful position
within Metro City, and he doesn't care who gets in his way.

NOW AVAILABLE!

www.glowingeyesmedia.com

The Wraith Dread Avenger of the Underworld #11

BIRDS OF THE LIVING DEAD

Frank Dirscherl

The dead are being re-animated, marching through Metro City, causing carnage throughout. Can The Wraith figure out what is going on, fight this undead menace, and find whomever is responsible? And what of the giant vultures plaguing the city? All this and more in this masterful tale of suspense and adventure.

COMING SOON!

www.glowingeyesmedia.com

Books of Judgment Book Three
RISING SON
Frank Dirscherl & Adam Oravec

Robert Latham, Metro City's pre-eminent businessman and entrepreneur. He's also the head of the largest crime cartel on the east coast, the insidious spider in the center of the city's web of evil. But how did he become this all-powerful figure? Growing up with nothing, he built his empire from the ground up, through strength, determination, and cold-blooded intimidation.

COMING SOON!

www.glowingeyesmedia.com

About the Type

Garamond is a group of many old-style serif typefaces, originally those designed by Parisian craftsman Claude Garamond and other 16th century French engravers, and now many modern revivals. Though his name was written as 'Garamont' in his lifetime, the typefaces are generally spelled 'Garamond'. **Garamond Normal**, used in this book, is one of those modern revivals.

Join FRANK DIRSCHERL and Glowing
Eyes Media on social media!

facebook.com/glowingeyesmedia

@glowingeyesmedia

instagram.com/glowingeyesmedia

@glowingeyesmedia.bsky.social

glowingeyesmedia.proboards.com

All Glowing Eyes Media, The Wraith and Starflame novels,
comics and merchandise can be obtained directly from the
Glowing Eyes Media website – www.glowingeyesmedia.com

Want to be The Wraith?

Well, it might be hard to actually *be* The Wraith, unless of course you, too, have been endowed with the power of the Eyes of Judgment. But you can certainly dress, drink and drive like him [*] (and you don't always have to be a millionaire to do so). See for yourselves.

The Wraith/Paul Sanderson wears:

- tailored clothing from Cad & the Dandy Tailors and Shirtmakers – www.cadandthedandy.co.uk
- bespoke footwear from Gaziano & Girling – www.gazianogirling.com
- watches from Héron (Marinor in Atlantic Blue), Erebus (Ascent 36mm in Enamel Black) and Jaeger-LeCoultre (Reverso Tribute Monoface Small Seconds in Opaline) -

    www.heronwatches.com/collections/marinor/products/marinor-atlantic-blue | www.erebuswatches.com/collections/ascent-36mm/products/ascent-36-black-enamel | www.jaeger-lecoultre.com/au-en/watches/reverso/reverso-tribute/reverso-tribute-small-seconds-q713842j
- Armani Code cologne from Giorgio Armani – www.giorgioarmanibeauty-usa.com/for-him-armani-code/for-him-armani-code,default,sc.html

drinks:

---

[*] Please note: Glowing Eyes Media does not condone drinking and driving. **All** adults, please always drink responsibly and **never** drink and drive

- Twinings Earl & Lady Grey tea – www.twinings.co.uk
- Vittoria coffee – www.vittoriacoffee.com/
- The Balvenie Scotch whisky – www.thebalvenie.com
- Armand de Brignac champagne – www.armanddebrignac.com
- Cosmopolitan cocktails

uses:

- Dell laptops – www.dell.com.au
- Chesterfield furniture from Abbey Furniture
  www.chesterfieldfurnituremelbourne.com.au
- wallets from Launer – www.launer.com
- a Samsung Galaxy J5 Pro cell phone –
  www.samsung.com/latin_en/smartphones/galaxy-j5-2017/SM-J530GZDITPA/

drives:

- a Rolls Royce Wraith – www.rolls-roycemotorcars.com/en-GB/wraith.html

And, if you're really eager to actually look like The Wraith—in full costume—then you can always head over to Xtreme Design FX and let Lance Coulter there make you an exact replica of the costume used for The Wraith motion picture – www.xtremedesignfx.com

HÉRON

Héron Marinor in Atlantic Blue - The Watch For Superheroes

GLOWING EYES MEDIA

EREBUS

Erebus Ascent 36mm in enamel black

GLOWINGEYESMEDIA

.

www.ingramcontent.com/pod-product-compliance
Lightning Source LLC
Chambersburg PA
CBHW071218260626
47162CB00004B/1344